Joyce

Love Well!

Velma Brinley Meritt
1 Cor. 13

River of Love

Velma Merritt

WESTBOW
PRESS
P R E S S
A DIVISION OF THOMAS NELSON

WestBow Press books may be ordered through booksellers or by contacting:

WestBow Press
A Division of Thomas Nelson
1663 Liberty Drive
Bloomington, IN 47403
www.westbowpress.com
1-(866) 928-1240

Because of the dynamic nature of the Internet, any web addresses or links contained in this book may have changed since publication and may no longer be valid. The views expressed in this work are solely those of the author and do not necessarily reflect the views of the publisher, and the publisher hereby disclaims any responsibility for them.

Any people depicted in stock imagery provided by Thinkstock are models, and such images are being used for illustrative purposes only. Certain stock imagery © Thinkstock.

ISBN: 978-1-4908-0319-7 (sc)
ISBN: 978-1-4908-0318-0 (hc)
ISBN: 978-1-4908-0320-3 (e)

Library of Congress Control Number: 2013913905

Printed in the United States of America.

WestBow Press rev. date: 8/7/2013

*Dedicated to Dale, who never
gave up when life got tough*

*Special thanks to my students
for their encouragement*

Chapter One

MEG PUSHED THE window button down. She needed air flowing around her, and at the moment, she didn't care that her hair would blow everywhere. The air conditioner's lack of cooperation in her ten-year-old car was exasperating. She had wanted this day to be perfect, but it seemed that everything that could go wrong had done just that. Murphy's Law was working perfectly for her today.

A brief power failure during the night had managed to turn off her morning alarm. Then Meg got stuck in road construction and had to wait in the subsequent traffic jam for forty-five minutes. To top it off her bare legs were sticking to the leather seats courtesy of the humid air blowing through the open window. Perspiration rolled down her back. Her long, dark blonde hair blew in a cascade around her head, making her feel more disheveled than rushed.

It's a good thing Bert won't mind my lateness, Meg thought. Her reputation as Miss Punctuality preceded her.

After working with high school students under the supervision of a less-than-friendly principal, Meg's last four summers at River's

View Resort were a joyful respite from the hectic school year. At River's View, Meg didn't have to worry about the ever-increasing load of paperwork, computer reports, teacher evaluations, or disrespectful and rebellious students. Nor did she have to worry about repelling the students who had crushes on her. She enjoyed working closely with her students, and having a good relationship with them meant getting to know them. She was adept at being friendly with the boys who needed help, but she had long ago learned to rebuff the hormonal young men's crushes.

Her students weren't the only ones Meg learned to discourage. She loved having a good time and frequently accepted dates, but she would date a man only a few times and then stop seeing him, refusing to allow herself to fall in love. *I can't*, she'd tell herself. Although she knew she'd hurt some of the guys, she refused to feel guilty. Her life was what it was, and there was nothing she could do about it. She was determined to remain single, because she did not want to bring her misfortune to any man.

Now, Meg blocked her thoughts about men and focused on pleasant thoughts of the resort. Bert often told her what an asset she was there. He allowed her to come later in the month than the other employees, because he knew she had to finish the school year. Besides, business was slow at the resort during the first week of June.

Twenty more minutes until I arrive, she thought, checking her watch. *At least I won't be very late.* She'd phoned to tell Bert she'd be a little late but had to leave a message, and it was only half past twelve. Her stomach growled, letting her know that lunch time had come and gone and that she had skipped breakfast.

The sun, at its full height, highlighted the Missouri hills she loved. Giant oaks, maples, and cottonwoods majestically stood in their early summer greenery. Pine trees pointed toward heaven. Mixed with the rocks walls, where highways had been blasted from the hills, the beauty of the area offset the crooked, narrow roads that led to the resort. When she saw a lookout area along the road, she wanted to stop and absorb the scenery—everything was green and lush—but conscious of the time, she kept to the road and pressed harder on the gas pedal.

At last she saw the gravel road leading to River's View. Despite the 11 mph speed limit on the road, Meg fairly flew over the last dusty mile. Now, she would not only be hot, but dust would be thick on her sticky skin.

When at last she pulled into the parking lot and opened her car door, she heard an unfamiliar, loud male voice, speaking with authority and agitation. She paused to listen.

"She had better be getting here. She's already almost an hour late, and we've got customers waiting to be picked up."

Meg heard Mattie, her friend for the past four summers, trying to calm the man down. "I'm sure she'll be here soon, Mr. Carson. Something must have happened, because Meg's always punctual."

Meg wiped the perspiration off her forehead as she hurriedly approached the open office door. This stranger was obviously talking about her. She glanced at her reflection in the window glass which did nothing to reassure her. Her clothes were wrinkled and wet with perspiration, which went right along with her windblown tresses. Her skin was covered in dust, and her usual smile was missing.

Might as well face the inevitable, Meg thought as she walked through the door.

"Meg!" Mattie cried. "Am I ever glad to see you! Did you have trouble? You look a bit undone."

Before Meg could reply, the man interjected, "So you're the Meg I've heard so much about." His grin belied his previous agitation. "I hate to rush you, but I need you to get the bus and pick up a group waiting at the river. Their canoe float is complete, and some of the folks are getting mighty impatient to be hauled back to the resort."

"But I just got here and haven't eaten …" Meg replied weakly.

"Look, miss, I don't have time to discuss this with you," the man snapped, his grin fading. "We have tourists waiting, so get going."

But Meg didn't budge. "I don't know you, but I take orders only from Bert, and besides, I don't drive the busses. My work is indoors."

"Can you drive a bus?" he asked tersely.

"Yes, but---"

"Look, I don't have time to argue with you," he said, taking Meg by the arm and escorting her back to the door.

"Bert's not here. I'm in charge, and right now I need a bus driver. You're all I've got. Now please—get going. The happy vacationers are waiting." He left no doubt that he was in charge and expected his orders to be obeyed.

"Where's Bert?" Meg asked as they stopped at the open bus door. He ignored her question and put his hand against her back persuasively ushering her through the door. *I'll do his bidding,* Meg decided, *but that stranger has not heard the last from me. I'll get to the bottom of this—and how dare he not let me eat lunch!*

As the stranger walked away, Meg started the bus. It sputtered several times and died. Her second try was successful. As she drove, she reached to pull the lever to shut the door and realized the door was missing.

"This bus is living up to the River's View bus reputation," Meg groaned. She wondered why Bert didn't purchase a newer model. She knew he was conservative by nature, but he expected every bus on the place to be used until it had breathed its last.

As if on cue, the bus sputtered and died. After a few tries, she revved the engine and eventually pulled into the designated meeting area for the canoe floaters. Those waiting for the bus had started ten miles upriver earlier in the day and had leisurely drifted down the Black River while dodging the even more relaxed tube floaters. The occasional set of rapids and wildlife kept the journey eventful and fun for the resort guests.

They clambered onto the bus, some obviously worn out and others ready for more action. As she watched a couple of them climb aboard, she wondered how long it would take before they realized how badly sunburned they were. *Don't city people know that sun reflects off the water and causes rapid sunburn?* Meg thought, shaking her head.

As the bus bounced back to the resort across gravel roads meant for only one lane of traffic, Meg glanced in her rearview mirror to check on her passengers and met the brightest blue eyes she'd ever seen.

The handsome gentleman saw her looking at him and grinned.

"Not bad driving … for a woman," Blue Eyes commented dryly.

Too bad his manners don't match his good looks, Meg thought. *Women can do almost anything a man can, despite what chauvinists like him think.*

When they got back to the resort, Blue Eyes spoke to her. "I don't have a partner to go tubing with tomorrow. Do you want to come with me?"

"No, thanks. I've got work to do," she answered as he exited the bus.

When everyone was off the bus, Meg parked it and hosed it clean of sand. She was thankful her trip was done and couldn't wait to get one of Ginger's three-layer sandwiches.

At the cafeteria, the delighted cook threw her arms around Meg's slender shoulders in greeting. "It's so good to see you! Did you just get here? I've got a three-layer left from lunch that's begging to be eaten."

Before Meg could utter a response, the sandwich was in her hands. As she was about to take her first anticipated bite, a voice called out, "Miss Green!"

"Hi, James," Mattie interjected. "I've got some leftovers if you want them."

It was the dictatorial man again who spoke directly to Meg. "I've got another group of floaters ready to be picked up in fifteen minutes. You're driver for the rest of the day. Please get with your work, and stop killing time here."

Meg turned away from him without saying a word, but she kept the sandwich in her hand, took a bite of it, and headed toward the bus. She held herself erect as she hurried, and James watched curiously as her exasperation with him evidenced itself in her stiff posture and deliberate walk. But what was he to do? She was the only one who could drive the bus this afternoon, and he had more folks checking in at any time.

Maybe I should leave right now, Meg seethed, *and let Mr. Bossy take care of things.* She didn't need this job, but she kept returning annually because past summers it had been relaxing and fun. She couldn't leave yet, though. She had to find out why this guy was here instead of Bert.

By the time she reached the river, Meg's frustration hadn't abated. The man had pushed her too far. She was hungry and tired after her hectic morning and long drive. But she didn't have time to indulge in self-pity—or in the rest of her sandwich, either—because she could hear the excited floaters heading toward the bus.

She smiled in spite of herself. They were certainly a grubby-looking group. The tube floaters had finally made it to their pickup point drifting in much slower than the canoes had. The children in the group were covered with sand and dirt. Some floaters were so sunburned that Meg wondered if they'd be participating in any river activities tomorrow. But they were happy and relaxed, which presented quite a contrast to Meg's own foul mood. For Bert's sake, however, she would act the part of a happy worker at River's View Resort.

The group piled into the bus with tubes, giant ice chests, towels, and very smelly bodies. Meg happily chatted with them, and the ride back to the resort was fun but bumpy. A group of teenagers in the back of the bus started singing a familiar song. "The wheels of the bus go round and round …" Giggles from the girls and laughter from the other tired passengers made the heat inside the bus bearable. Meg sped down the narrow gravel road as though she'd been driving the old school bus for years. She deliberately took a few low spots faster than was necessary so she could make the ride more memorable for the passengers. The resort had the reputation of having challenging bus rides. She wanted some of the tourists to buy the T-shirt emblazoned with "I survived the bus ride at River's View Resort."

As the guests were disembarking, many courteously thanked her. She was truly glad for the experience until she heard sounds of an upset stomach coming from a small child toward the back. "Oh, no," she murmured as she went to see if she could help the mother with her sick child. Meg felt a bit of remorse for making the ride so bouncy.

"I'm so sorry," the mother commented. "Julie has motion

sickness, and I didn't think I would need her medicine. I'll clean the bus."

"Take care of your little girl. It's my job to clean things in here."

The smell coming from the back of the bus was repugnant as Meg drove toward the parking area that held the hoses. She hoped the hose would be long enough to spray the mess out the emergency door. No such luck—she had to fill a bucket with water and pour it over the floor several times so she could sweep out the vomit.

As he brought his horse into the stable, James Carson, riding back from overseeing another resort project, saw Meg cleaning the bus. Her shoulder-length, dark blonde hair blew in the breeze. He noticed the yellow shorts and V-necked white blouse Meg wore emphasized her femininity. She appeared soft and vulnerable, but James had already seen her spark and knew fire was hidden behind the calm exterior.

As she worked, her flip-flop slipped off, and she jumped from the bus to retrieve it. She was totally unaware she was being observed by her new boss, just as she was oblivious to the fact that she had brought a grin to his face and a determination to his heart to learn more about this feisty lady Bert was so fond of.

By six o'clock that evening, Meg had made three trips to the river to pick up either canoe or tube floaters returning from their day of adventure on the Black River. She sat at the gravel bar waiting for her fourth load and wondered who was more tired—her or the happy floaters coming from a busy but relaxing day. As she waited for the canoes to come, she closed her eyes and prayed, *Lord, I thought I was supposed to come here this summer, but things have gotten off to a rocky start. Help me to know if I was wrong about working at the resort again. If I should go back home ...*" She began to doze. When she awoke a few minutes later, she saw that a pickup truck and canoe trailer from the resort had joined her in waiting for the canoes.

Laughing, happy voices drew her attention to the river's edge. "Look, Mr. Carson! Look! See what I got today!" A little girl in a bright red swimming suit was running toward James Carson with a rusty can in her hand.

"What have you got there, Lisa?" He bent to look into the treasure she held. "Well, I'll be. It looks to me like you caught yourself some fish."

"Don't you kid me," the youngster exclaimed. "You know they're not fish—they're only minnows."

"Aren't minnows fish?" he teased.

"Yes, but my minnows are different. I'm going to put them in my aquarium with the guppies."

"I think you'd better ask your mom and dad about that," he reasoned. "Your dad might want to put them in a minnow bucket to catch other fish."

Meg watched the man, who had been impatient with her, walk with little Lisa's hand held tightly in his own. *How could Mr. Carson be so tender and compassionate with a child yet so irritable with me?*

A few minutes later, James began hauling the canoes up the river bank to toss them into place on the trailer racks as though they were practically weightless. In a T-shirt and cutoff jeans, his tan muscles glistened with sweat. It was obvious he had already spent much time outdoors this summer. His rugged good looks showed the firmness with which he had spoken to Meg, yet there was uncommon gentleness as he spoke with little Lisa.

He was taller than Meg was—probably about six foot two, she guessed. Although he looked to be in his late twenties, no wedding band was visible on his left hand. As he pushed his dark hair from his face, Meg stared in appreciation at his muscles, thinking *"Quite a hunk of a man"*.

<hr />

"I'm famished, gang. Let's eat." Meg was the first of the resort staff to get in line at the cafeteria. "All I've had to eat today is a sandwich, and I need some food in this tummy." She patted her stomach as if to emphasize the point.

"Miss Green, you will need your energy this summer, so see that you get three well-balanced meals a day. Ginger's a mighty good cook, and from the looks of you, it wouldn't hurt you to put on a pound or two." She had heard that voice too many times today, and knew it was James taunting her before she turned to look at him.

Meg thought he was teasing, but she wasn't sure. She just wanted to eat a decent meal in the company of her fellow workers. Suddenly angry and irritable, she flared, "I would have had at least two good meals today, but you wouldn't let me eat. When I came to get a three-layer from Ginger, you rushed me to pick up another group of floaters. I had to gobble it down. I can't do my best work without decent food."

Suddenly contrite, James said, "Is that why you were so tired you dozed while waiting for the last group of floaters to get back?"

Meg turned crimson. *He would have to tell everyone that I fell asleep on the job.* The other workers had respected her in the past. As she glanced around the room, she noticed they didn't seem to disrespect her but were enjoying the verbal sparring between the two of them. Without another word, she walked from the room without bothering to get her supper. Meg hadn't yet unpacked and was now glad of it. *I'm going back home,* she decided. *No way can I put up with Mr. Carson this summer. And no one has said when Bert is coming back.*

Meg paced the cabin floor until exhaustion overcame her confusion. She decided to go to bed early. She was almost ready for bed when she heard a knock on the cabin door. "Who's there?"

"James Carson."

"Just a minute. I was getting ready for bed and am in my pjs."

"Hurry up. I want to talk to you. Throw a robe on."

Oh, that man! she fumed. *Hasn't anyone ever taught him patience?*

When she finally came to the door, James stared at her. "May I come in?" He was clutching a box.

Her training in proper etiquette came to the forefront. "Oh, I'm sorry." She ushered him inside and motioned for him to take a seat on the wooden folding chair. She sat on the edge of the bed, and when she looked up, he was watching her. His eyes quickly took in her bare feet and soft blue robe and then rested on her face.

Although the spark of irritability had not left her green eyes, he could tell she was tired.

"I guess I've been pretty hard on you today. I'm sorry, Monica."

Meg's eyes narrowed as she looked directly into his eyes.

"Monica. How did you know my name is Monica? No one—and I mean no one—calls me that."

"Monica Elizabeth Green. Meg for short. Age twenty-six. Height, five foot six. Weight 118. Green eyes, dark blonde hair. Occupation, high school teacher. Marital status, single."

"So you've read the information about me in the files. "Why did you come to my cabin?"

"I came to apologize for being so impatient today. I should have driven the bus myself and given you time to settle into your cabin. My morning hadn't gone well, and I took my frustration out on you." He opened the box he carried and took out a plate of food—a pork chop, fried potatoes, corn on the cob, and a hunk of watermelon. "I brought this as a peace offering. Going without food isn't going to help you gain any weight. Now eat up so I won't feel so guilty." His grin had a boyish charm to it.

Meg glanced once at the plate and then did just as he said.

"Maybe I should have brought extra food," he joked as Meg swallowed the last bite.

Ignoring his comment, Meg asked, "Where's Bert, and why are you here?"

"Whoa, one question at a time. I guess you haven't heard about Bert's accident. He had the palomino up on the ridge a couple of weeks ago when a snake spooked his horse. Bert went down the cliff. The workers didn't know there was a problem until the palomino came back to the stable a few hours after Bert left. After a long search, the guys found him, unconscious and with a broken back." Meg gasped and listened more intently as James continued. "He's in the hospital in Poplar Bluff and will be for some time. When he got well enough to make a phone call, he asked me to come and run the resort this summer. Bert's been like a grandfather to me, and the earnings I made here at River's View are what allowed me to get through college debt free. I owe him big time."

"You mean … you're the Jimmy he talks about all the time? Bert always said what a nice guy Jimmy was. It's nice to finally meet you." She offered her hand for a handshake. "I'm sorry," she apologized. "Today has not been a good day for me either, and I've been really grouchy too." She blushed at the realization he was included in the grouchy comment.

He laughed with her admission and hoped they had cleared the air of hard feelings. "You can call me James. Nobody but Bert calls me Jimmy, and I sure don't want you calling me Mr. Carson like you've done all day. It makes me feel old, and I'm just a couple years older than you."

James and Meg talked a few more minutes before he excused himself and vanished into the night. Before she closed the door, she took a deep, satisfying breath of the smoke coming from the guest campfires. The memory lingered as she made her way to bed.

Meg, now content with the situation at the resort, determined that she too would help Bert this summer. She forgot all about leaving the next day and drifted into a sound sleep.

***

Meg had assumed she would be back at her former jobs as public-relations person and bookkeeper in the general store, but when James handed out the daily work assignments the next morning, she was given the task of filling up inner tubes for floating.

"Think you can handle that?" His slight grin seemed to be issuing a challenge so she quickly replied, "Of course. Who couldn't?"

She didn't know what James was doing, but she was going to take anything he threw her way. If he wanted to challenge her ability, she'd show him she could do everything at the resort. Her stubborn streak was proving to be as big as his. She'd do this job so well that he'd have to find her something else to do.

The tube room behind the general store would have been claustrophobic if not for the wide window that opened to dispense the tubes. The rest of the time it was air conditioned and free from hassles. She would have an easy, relaxing day compared to yesterday.

Meg grabbed a box of empty tubes the size of truck tires and began filling the first one with air. After airing up several, she seated herself on three tubes stacked precariously on top of one another. She pulled the air hose toward her and flipped an empty tube onto her lap. She leaned back casually on the stack of tubes and let her legs dangle over the edge.

After several more of the tubes were filled, she began to daydream about floating down the river on a lazy afternoon. She wished she could do just that. One glance out the window made her realize the day was perfect for lazily floating along the usually slow-moving, clear Black River. Thinking about the occasional rapids and dodging the rocks sticking up from the river's bottom under the old bridge brought her light laughter to the forefront.

"Do you always laugh to yourself?"

Who else but James would come in and startle her? She tried to jump off the tubes but instead succeeded in upsetting her precarious stack. She landed ungracefully on the floor, which made James roar with laughter.

"You have no right to come behind a person and scare her half to death!"

"I just came to see if you would watch the front desk for a while since you're already so close. We've got a busted water pipe in the campground, and nobody else around here knows how to fix it. I've got to get on it before we get a puddle big enough to be a swimming pool."

Without waiting for her answer, he was out the door. In a little over an hour, James was back.

Floaters were waiting in line at the window to get their tubes for the afternoon float when Meg returned to the tube room.

"I want a real *big* one," a young voice hollered.

"Hello there," Meg said. "Are you Lisa?"

"How did you know my name? You're new."

"I heard you talking about your minnows yesterday. Are you going to put them with your guppies?"

"Nope. Dad said it won't work. I can just have minnows at the river. At home I can have my guppies. My minnows have to stay in my daddy's minnow bucket."

"Well, that will make them a special treat while you're here. Now let's talk about that tube. I'm afraid if you get a big one, you'll fall right through the hole in the middle. How would you like this one that's just your size?"

"You sound like my mommy," little Lisa said disgustedly. "Don't want that one. I want a big one like Daddy."

It took patience, but the child left with the smaller tube, and Meg breathed a sigh of relief.

After the floaters had gotten their tubes for the day, Meg filled the remaining new tubes and then got the bright yellow paint to put the RVR initials on them. Tubes frequently got away from their owners, and with other lodges, campgrounds, and resorts also using the Black River, having a way to identify a tube was a necessity. She wouldn't admit, not even to herself, but Meg was just a bit disappointed when James didn't check on her before her shift was complete.

Chapter Two

*M*EG KNEW SOMETHING was wrong when she glanced at Chuck. The sixteen-year-old worker's downcast face was a certain giveaway to his emotions.

Chuck walked directly to James. "Sir, I lost the canoe trailer."

"Excuse me? Say that again—I don't think I heard you right."

"I said I lost the canoe trailer."

After taking a deep sigh, James asked how he'd managed to lose it.

"I forgot to check the hitch. When I heard it click, I didn't check to make sure it had caught and locked."

"Well, Chuck, you've got a problem. I don't have time to help you this afternoon, so you're going to have to figure out a way to get it back. Trailers aren't cheap, so be careful and don't damage it further. See if you can find someone around here who's not busy and have him go with you to get it. Next time, check the hitch before you pull a trailer."

James had left Chuck standing in the room, embarrassed. Meg walked up behind him and put her hand on his shoulder.

"Come on, Chuck. I'm finished with my work, so I can go with you."

"Do you know how to get it? It slid down a little hill."

"I think between the two of us, we can figure it out. Let's go."

Once outside Meg suggested they take the 4x4 instead of the truck that Chuck had been driving. She knew the four-wheel drive would be needed to pull the trailer back onto the road.

When they got back to the place of the accident, the two of them were able to position the trailer so it could be hooked to the trailer ball of the 4x4 when the vehicle backed down the hill. Meg waited in the road to stop oncoming traffic as Chuck made several attempts to line up the truck and trailer. Finally successful, he pulled the trailer onto the road, stopped, and let Meg climb in.

Chuck was all grins. "Boy, am I glad I got that back! Getting it lined up right was a lot tougher than I imagined it'd be."

At supper that evening, James walked up to the table where Meg and Mattie were sitting. "Do you ladies mind if I join you?" he asked as he set his tray down. "How did your day go?"

"James, you're just the man I've wanted to see," Mattie said. "Can I work the concession stand all summer? I enjoy dishing out ice cream and talking to the kids."

James slid the chair out and raised his leg over the seat to sit down.

"If you want it, you've got it. I'm still trying to place workers where they will be the most productive. Happy workers accomplish more. How about you, Meg? Would you like to inflate tubes all summer?"

Meg was about to answer "No way" when she caught the twinkle in his eye. "Sure, why not?" she said with a smirk. "It'd give me a real vacation from brain duty—not much thinking involved in filling tubes."

As the three of them ate, he spoke to Meg.

"Sorry to disappoint you, but Bert's told me you're good at the desk in the general store. I need you to keep the customers happy and do the bookkeeping for the folks coming in. It's really important to me that Bert's customers have a good experience this summer, and I'm counting on you to see that they do."

Meg took a bite of her hamburger and complemented James.

"You were good with Chuck this afternoon. You didn't over-react, and you tried to teach him responsibility at the same time. Some guys would have lost their temper at a kid for losing a trailer. Does it come naturally, or have you had experience in working with people?"

"A little of both, I guess. Usually, I'm pretty laid back, but now that I'm in charge at the resort for the summer, I feel responsible to keep things going for Bert. I've had a few psychology courses in college and seminary, so I plan to use what I learned on the staff. Chuck was the first. I was too ill-tempered with him."

James dipped his spoon into his chocolate pudding.

"So …" she teased, "how would your professors suggest you handle me this summer?"

"You need to work so hard you don't have time to get mad at me. And you'll need some variety in your life, which means you'll need someone to date."

Meg rolled her eyes and faked a cough.

Despite knowing he was referring to himself, she innocently asked, "Oh, who's around here to date? Chuck's too young for me."

"Oh, I don't know. Maybe some old grouch that starves cute teachers the first day they get to the resort."

Her grin said yes, but she shook her head and laughed as she left James sitting at the table with Mattie.

———

The pounding on her door awakened her. Meg squinted at the clock beside her bed and saw it wasn't quite five in the morning. Who would be waking her at this ungodly hour? Sleepily, she grabbed her robe and shuffled to the door.

James stood there with a Cheshire-cat grin. "We've got a group of floaters coming in at six. If you want any breakfast, you'd better hurry, or you won't get to eat with me. Since I didn't see your light on, I figured I'd be your alarm clock."

Meg stared at him trying to decide whether to smile at his enthusiasm or ring his neck for waking her so early.

"Are you awake?" he questioned as he reached to give her shoulder a gentle shake.

"Sorry. It's not every day I get awakened personally."

"See you at breakfast as soon as those green eyes are ready to face the day."

Meg closed the door but heard James laugh. It wasn't until she stood before the mirror that she saw the humor in the situation. She definitely had bed-head. Her hair was standing out in several directions, and the mascara she'd forgotten to remove the previous night had left her with football-player smudges under her eyes.

She lumbered to the shower, which would wake her up and remedy her looks.

After Meg had checked in the guests and escorted them to the buses, she went back to the general store to compute the morning's receipts. She was envious of the group because she hadn't gotten to stick a toe in the river since she'd been at the resort. Usually by the second day, Meg would have already been floating at least for an hour in the evening, but this year there hadn't been time.

Everything was different with Bert's replacement here. *No, not everything*, she reasoned. *Only the boss was different.* She couldn't expect him to do things like Bert did. Everyone had different ways of accomplishing tasks.

This morning she was having difficulty getting her mind off James. His touch this morning had been gentle as he shook her shoulder. She really admired the way he was doing everything possible to help their friend Bert. And she loved the twinkle in his eyes when she suspected he was up to a little mischief. And the dimple ... he had only one dimple, which fascinated her.

She was lost in her daydreaming and didn't realize James had come in until a work-hardened hand touched her arm.

"Why are you smiling?" he asked.

"I was just daydreaming about the river. In past years I would have already gotten some float time. You know Bert believes in his workers having some fun too." He asked her to see if any more groups were coming today. She saw the register and said, "Townsend, group of ten. Tubes."

"Get changed. We're going canoeing."

Meg countered, "I wasn't hinting for you to take me."

"I'll get Sue to watch the desk and will meet you by the truck in ten minutes."

With that said James was out the door and headed to get the truck and canoe trailer.

Meg showed up in shorts, sneakers and a cover-up, but James could see her swim suit strap tied below her pony tail. Swim time was coming, and he was glad he had pulled swim trunks under his jeans shorts that morning.

They drove through the campground to a rocky beach where tube floaters could get into the cold, slowly moving water.

James stepped to the trailer and put his shoulders under the highest canoe to hoist it up before letting it drop to the beach. As he pulled it toward the water, Meg asked, "How do you guys lift those canoes like they're made of paper?"

"Muscles, my dear. Just muscles," he joked as he launched the canoe.

"Take the front, Meg. Don't lead me astray, and watch out for rocks right under the surface of the water. Don't let the rapids sneak up on you, and—"

"This isn't my first time in a canoe. I know how to float. You get us over the rapids without flipping the canoe, and we will be fine."

"Okay ... I forgot you've been here every summer for several years. I guess you know what you're doing." James looked as though he didn't quite believe her.

As Meg jumped in, the canoe rocked beneath her sneaker-clad feet. Still dressed in her white cover-up, she realized it wouldn't be long before the sun would warm the day enough to remove it—the forecast was for a hot June day. She already wanted to jump into the water and feel its coolness. She'd wait, and maybe she would get to swim a little and not have to work the entire day.

James had brought hooks for cleaning the river and trash bags to put the litter.

"We'll float until we see litter on the river bottom. If we can't get it in the deeper areas from the canoe, we can dive if we need to do so." James handed Meg a black garbage bag and a bamboo rod with a large grasping hook on the end of it. She laid them beside her and picked up the paddle he had given her earlier.

"I can manage the canoe. You keep your eye out for litter," James commented.

Meg was glad to comply with the order. She felt a little like Huck Finn today and didn't want to work.

The early morning floaters were long gone, so Meg and James had the river to themselves. For a long while, they drifted slowly in companionable silence. Occasionally, Meg would hook an aluminum soda can and bring it to her trash bag, but mostly she sat enjoying the scenery and listening to the gentle ripple of the water as it ran over the rocks. When she looked at the bank and saw how high the spring floods had come, she spotted some debris in the lower overhanging limbs. When she mentioned getting it, he said they weren't going to worry about the high stuff.

"Hey, Meg, hook that shoe." She had almost missed the sneaker.

"Have you ever wondered what the owner of the shoe did with the other one?" she questioned. "Every year I see a single shoe on the bottom. I've never seen a pair."

"I'm guessing he pitched the other shoe, or we'll pick it up farther downstream. Grab your paddle, Meg. I hear rapids."

Meg put her paddle in the river just in time to help James maneuver without a hitch through the quickly moving water.

"Nice going," he said. "You've just proven that you really have been in a canoe before. Say, you're not a river rat, are you?"

"Hardly, I'd never been in a canoe until I started coming to the resort, but when I tried it, I loved it so much that I float as often as I can now. I like the tranquility of the river on days like this, when it's not crowded with other floaters. The clean smell added to the trickling water is really relaxing. I even like to watch the dragonflies playing on the water. They seem worry-free."

"That's how I feel about it too. We're coming to the swimming hole around the bend. Are you warm enough for a swim? We've been working for almost an hour."

"Sure. I've been waiting for a chance to dive in."

"Let me check the hole first. I haven't been in it yet this year, and I want to make sure the spring floods didn't fill it up. I don't relish breaking either of our necks."

Around the bend, they dragged the canoe to the gravel bar. James swam underwater to check the depth of the swimming hole and okayed it. Meg started to join James in the water when he called to her, "Aren't you going to take off your cover-up?"

She rushed back through the water, splashing and giggling like one of her teenage students. She tossed the cover-up toward the canoe and ran back through the water.

James had come from the deeper water to grab her hand and run with her until the water was deep enough to swim. Suddenly, James pulled Meg underwater.

"James Carson! You're asking for it!" Meg sputtered as she surfaced and wiped her face.

"And just what are you going to do? Do you really think you can pull me under?"

She started toward him, slipped on a mossy rock, and went under again. Instead of coming up, she swam underwater and grabbed James' legs. He went splashing face forward.

For half an hour they played, until finally Meg said, "Enough! You've nearly drowned me half a dozen times just because I got you once. Back to the canoe," she shouted, "or we'll never get the river clean today."

"Slave driver," James said under his breath.

As they prepared to push off, James said, "Your back is getting red. Did you forget your sunscreen?"

"I covered everything but my back. I was going to have Mattie do it, but I ran out of time."

"Hand me your lotion. Bert will skin me alive if I let his favorite worker get burned to a crisp."

Obediently, Meg handed James the lotion. His touch was gentle as he smoothed it over her shoulders and back. When his hands moved back to her shoulders, he turned her around to face him. She saw the look of a forthcoming kiss and was thrilled. She wanted James to like her. *No, James couldn't like me,* she thought. *Could he?*

He stared at her without comment, noticing her confusion, and wondered if it was because she didn't like him or if she was unsure of his motives. He dropped his eyes and picked up the paddle. "Let's get to it," he said.

She turned away from him hoping her disappointment didn't betray her.

Who is this woman? James wondered. *Something's troubling her.* He hoped he would learn the answer, but he knew it wouldn't be today.

The silence of the morning's float continued, but the camaraderie was gone, as each of them was lost in private thoughts.

I've got to get away from him, Meg told herself. *I might have to work with him, but I'll never go anywhere with him again. I know he likes me, but I won't let his growing feelings for me get beyond this day.*

Meg turned toward the sound of off-road vehicles coming near.

"Is something wrong? You're frowning."

"Just too much sun, I guess," she fibbed. "It's my first time out this year."

"We're about to a landing anyway. We can finish cleaning the lower half of the river another day."

After they dragged the canoe to a nearby gravel bar, James loaded the canoe onto the waiting trailer. They got into the parked truck to make the short drive back to the resort. When they arrived at the parking lot, Meg exited and headed in the direction of her cabin. "Wait up, Meg! I forgot something."

Meg stopped but didn't turn around. James took her by surprise when he stepped in front of her and gave her a quick, gentle kiss.

"I forgot to kiss you. Thanks for a fun morning."

The corners of Meg's mouth turned upward in a soft smile when she looked into his bright eyes. What she saw was unexpected and surely would complicate her summer.

Chapter Three

$\mathcal{M}$EG NEEDED TO hurry if she was going to get to the chapel by 7:00. During the tourist season, the only church in town held an early service for workers of the resorts along the Black River.

The first praise song already had begun when Meg slipped into an empty seat. It wasn't until she looked around her that she realized James was sitting only a few feet away. She had successfully avoided him for several days and now had inadvertently blown her resolve to stay away from him.

Concentrate, Meg, she told herself. She repeatedly admonished herself throughout the service, but by the time the service ended, she hardly knew a word Pastor Rex had spoken, and she definitely had not worshipped. She was aware, however, of every tiny movement James had made during the service, which further distracted her.

As they were exiting the chapel, James was directly behind her, also waiting to shake hands with Pastor Rex. He spoke to Meg. "His text is one of my favorites. What did you think about it?"

Meg turned to greet someone else so she wouldn't have to

answer his question. She didn't want James to know she hadn't been paying attention to the text. When she again looked toward him, he continued speaking. "When things seem impossible with us, God has an opportunity to work. I'm going to be thinking on his topic during this week. There are some situations in my life that seem pretty impossible, and I'd sure like God to work in them." His direct look and subsequent smile was her undoing.

She looked away from him for the second time within only a few seconds.

"Why didn't you ride to chapel in the van with the rest of us?" James asked. "There wasn't much point in your wasting gas when we were all coming to the same place."

"I got up too late," Meg responded. She didn't want to tell him she had deliberately avoided him.

He gave her arm a gentle squeeze. "It must have been beauty sleep you were getting because you look beautiful this morning."

As shivers raced through her from his touch, she could not hide the smile that came with his compliment.

At supper that evening, James walked straight to her table. "I'm going to Poplar Bluff tomorrow afternoon to see Bert. I've checked the schedule, and things don't look too busy, so I wondered if you would like to go too. I know he'd sure be glad to see you."

James had decided Meg was deliberately avoiding him. It had taken him several hours to think of something they could do together that she wouldn't be able to resist. Since he knew she wanted to see with her own two eyes how Bert was doing, he had cunningly laid out what he hoped would be an irresistible plan.

"I'd love to see Bert, but—"

"Meg, why have you been avoiding me?" James broke in. "If you see me coming, you go the opposite direction. I know I offended you the first day, but I've apologized and tried to make up for it. Surely it's not that difficult to be around me."

"James, I … I'm not avoiding you. It's just that I don't want to get involved with anyone."

When James burst out laughing, Meg drew back as though she had been slapped.

"And what's so funny?" she snapped.

"One quick kiss, and you think I want to get serious. Why don't you just relax and enjoy the time we can spend together? The future will take care of itself."

"All right," Meg sighed in resignation. "I'll go with you, but stop laughing. The other workers are staring at us."

"Sorry, but I couldn't figure out what I'd done to make you try so hard to avoid me. I was beginning to get an inferiority complex from you."

"It's not you. It's just that I can't ..." She hesitated, not sure how to say what she wanted to tell him.

"In case I don't see you before it's time to leave tomorrow," James said, sensing her discomfort, "meet me in the parking lot at 1:00."

Meg nodded, though she dreaded the long drive. Still, it would be so good to see Bert. She wanted to assure herself that he was going to be all right.

"I hope you don't mind riding in the van," James said the next afternoon as they were preparing to leave for the hospital visit. "It's more comfortable than my Model T."

"You've got a Model T?" Meg quickly glanced around the parking lot but didn't see one.

"I wish! My car is old enough that it seems like one. It doesn't have air conditioning, and the van does. Bert told me to use the van like it was my own this summer, so I'm going to do just that. It's not every day I get to escort a pretty girl to Poplar Bluff."

When she got in the van, James reached over her to get the seat belt she had not fastened. "I like my passengers to be safe," he commented as he buckled her into the seat. "Besides if you're strapped in, you can't get away from me when I slow down or stop."

The scent of his aftershave lingered after he moved away from her and made her long for his closeness. As they pulled out of the parking spot, he turned down the radio.

"Don't do that for me," Meg said. "I like Southern gospel music."

"That's a switch. Most women your age don't like it."

"I like all kinds of music, not just one genre."

"I thought you'd like the long-hair stuff."

"Why would you think that?"

"You're pretty serious—almost like something is eating at you. But actions can be wrong. Guess I misjudged you."

That launched them into a discussion about music, and they learned they had much the same taste. Without realizing it, Meg was enjoying herself.

"That road sign read six more miles. This trip has gone quickly," James commented. "It must be your pleasant company. Do you want to see Bert by yourself for a while, or is it okay if I come in the room at the same time?"

"I don't have anything private to say to him. I just want to see for myself how he's doing."

When they got to the hospital, James let Meg exit at the front door and asked her to meet him in the entrance waiting room after he parked.

"I don't have a gift for Bert. Could we go by the gift shop?" Meg asked after James entered the building.

They wandered through the gift shop and picked out a potted plant in a wicker basket. "He'll like something simple. This will be good for the general store when he gets out of the hospital," Meg reasoned.

As she started to pay the cashier, James stopped her.

"I haven't gotten him anything either. It can be from both of us." He pulled out his wallet and paid for the plant and then scribbled on the get-well card, "James and Meg."

As they searched for Bert's room, Meg handed James some bills. "Here's my portion of the tab."

He waved it away. "Put your money away. It's already handled."

"You put both names on the card, so I'll pay my half," Meg insisted.

James sighed heavily and pursed his lips. "I said I'd pay, Meg. Let me be a gentleman."

With his chauvinist attitude, she decided it would be useless to argue but snapped, "Have it your way then, but we both know the plant is from you—not the two of us."

James wanted to argue, but they had reached Bert's room.

Bert was elated to see them. "Meg … Jimmy. Am I ever glad to see some familiar faces. Come here and give this old man a hug."

"It's so good to see you," Meg gushed as she reached to hug him. "How are you doing?"

"'Bout what you'd expect, I guess. My back hurts a bunch. Sure would rather be at the resort. How'd you like the surprise of this here handsome guy coming to my rescue?"

Meg smiled and gave Bert's arm a warm squeeze. "It was a surprise. When I first arrived at the resort, I couldn't figure out where you were."

"I don't know what I would have done without you, boy," he said with gratitude to James. "Meg's as dependable as I told you, ain't she, Jimmy? Yes sir-ee, there's nobody like Meg—always so happy and cheerful for our customers. She's the best PR person I've ever had."

Bert spoke quickly, not giving them time to respond. He didn't see the questioning look James sent Meg's direction when Bert commented on her happy attitude.

James wondered where that attitude had gone this summer and said, "Meg hasn't been acting—"

"Well, of course not," Bert interrupted. "She doesn't act, boy. She's the real thing—always happy. I've 'bout claimed her as my granddaughter, like I hoodwinked you into being a grandson a few years back. 'Course, she's got her own grandparents, but it never hurts to have an extra one."

"James brought you this plant," Meg said, taking the plant from James and placing it on Bert's bedside table.

The look James gave her told her she was pushing her luck by saying the plant was from him alone. She was sure she'd hear about it later.

Bert offered his thanks and then looked at the card. "James

and Meg," he read. "I like that. After you guys catch me up on all the news from the resort, I'll pay for your supper at that fancy restaurant downtown. I heard tell that's supposed to be a good eatin' spot."

"No, Bert," Meg quickly responded. "We need to get right back to the resort."

"We don't have to go right back," James rebutted. "Remember, I told you the afternoon wasn't busy. That's why we could come."

"Sorry, I ... I just ... I forgot," she stammered as her eyes dropped to the floor.

Bert's eyes narrowed as he watched Meg carefully. "She always was too conscientious. Get my wallet out of the drawer, Jimmy."

James did as requested, and Bert handed him two bills. "If you have anything left after paying for supper, take her to the picture show. She probably needs to relax a little. She looks a little uptight to me."

Meg chewed nervously on her lower lip. Bert's good nature was getting her into trouble. Why had she ever agreed to come with James? Now she'd end up spending not only the afternoon but the evening with him too.

She breathed a sigh of relief when Bert started asking about the resort, and the rest of the visit went quickly.

As James and Meg were walking toward the hospital exit, she said, "I want to go back to River's View."

James stopped her right in the middle of the corridor. "Meg, you are going to have dinner with me whether you like it or not. Bert's paid for it, and we're not going to disappoint him. If you force yourself, you can put up with my company for an evening." The firm grip he held on her elbow told her he was determined to do as Bert had asked. When he saw she wasn't going to resist, his hand loosened, and he gave her a brotherly pat on the back. "That's better," James said when Meg nodded in agreement. "Now give me a pretty smile."

Meg was waiting for James to remember what Bert said about her always smiling and being happy. She was certain he'd ask what had happened to her this summer, but he didn't bring up the subject.

The restaurant Bert had sent them to was luxurious for a town the size of Poplar Bluff. The plush red carpet and huge crystal chandeliers immediately caught Meg's artistic eye.

"Pretty place, isn't it?" James commented.

"Wow, I'll say it is!" Meg agreed. "I love these chandeliers." Then in a conspiratorial whisper, she asked, "Do you suppose simple folks like resort workers can eat in a place so uppity?"

"We'll give it a try, and see if they serve us," he joked.

The hostess seated them by a window that overlooked a fountain with gently cascading water.

"It's absolutely lovely," Meg observed. Then she seriously asked James, "What do you suppose it would look like if we emptied a bottle of dishwashing detergent in it?"

"Bubbles would be everywhere!" he laughed picturing the scene in his mind. "We could even add food coloring to the detergent and get colored bubbles."

Before long, both were enjoying themselves. When the waitress came to take their order, James ordered a T-bone steak with baked potato, while Meg asked for the cordon bleu. When their salads arrived, James placed his hand over Meg's hand. Startled, she started to withdraw hers, but realized James wasn't being flirtatious—he had bowed his head and was praying aloud, giving thanks to God for their food.

As quickly as he had taken her hand, he withdrew it and began eating. Meg wondered if he had made the gesture spontaneously and unconsciously.

"You pray before your meals at home, don't you?" Meg questioned.

"Yes, I guess it's an old habit. Seems like my food goes down better if I ask God to bless it first. Tell me about your family."

"Bill used to go on and on with his mealtime prayer," Meg said. "He'd thank God for everything—the dog, cat, sun, silverware, plates—everything except the food. Dad would say, 'Bill, don't forget the food.' Then he'd add, 'And the food too, God. Thanks for it 'cause I don't want to be hungry. Amen.'"

"Bill's your brother?" he asked.

Meg nodded. "You might know him. He's going to the same seminary you mentioned you attend."

"Bill Green ..." he pondered. "Of course! I've had a couple of classes with him. The world's a small place, isn't it? Here I am, eating with Bill's little sister."

"Bill's older sister," she corrected.

"You look younger. Tell me about your parents," James continued.

"My dad owns his own construction business. His work comes and goes with the economy. Since he mostly builds houses, things have been slow lately."

"That beats what my dad did. He worked for a mining company. He worked long hours underground and had little to show for it when we moved to Missouri thirteen years ago. What about your mom—does she work outside the home?" he asked.

"No, Mom is ..." Meg hesitated for a moment and then said, "Mom stays home."

"That's good. I always wished my mom could have been home when I got home from school, but she wasn't. She chose to work, which is okay too. You know the old saying, 'Different strokes for different folks.' It didn't hurt us any."

"Does she still work?"

James shook his head sadly. "She was an office assistant—and a good one, I've been told. She died last winter."

"I'm sorry. I shouldn't have asked about her."

"Don't be sorry. I loved her and liked to pick her brain. She was a smart woman. She'd evidently had cancer for a long time before it bothered her enough to see a doctor. By the time the cancer was diagnosed, it had advanced too far for treatment to be successful."

"Why'd she wait so long to go to the doctor?"

"I imagine because of Amy. She needed a lot of extra care, and Mom insisted she would not put her in a home. Mom would ignore her health to insure that Amy was happy."

"Amy's your sister?"

"Yes ... she went to the special school district all year because of multiple handicaps. That freed Mom to work during the day, but in the evenings, Amy required a lot of attention."

"Who takes care of her now?"

"We had to put her in a home when Mom died. Dad was never as good with her as Mom was. He couldn't cope with her multiple problems. Strange, isn't it? Some people can cope with problems and some can't. But Amy's adjusting well. I saw her right before I came to the resort this summer. Dad gets lonesome for Mom. He misses Amy too and goes to see her almost every day. I think he feels guilty that he can't care for her physically like Mom could."

Meg was surprised when she glanced at her watch and realized two hours had passed. She had enjoyed talking to James, despite her earlier objection to spending time with him.

The waitress appeared at their table to ask, "Would you like some vanilla ice cream bon-bons covered with chocolate? They're served over dry ice and are our specialty."

When James saw Meg's face light up at the dessert description, he said, "We might as well."

Brought to their table in a cloud of rising mist, the bon-bons were delicious.

"Oh, the calories," Meg groaned as she tasted the first one.

"You can afford them. Enjoy it while you can. Tomorrow we'll take a trail ride, and you can bounce the calories off."

When they finished their dessert, they decided to drop by the hospital again and tell Bert about their evening.

"Hi again, 'ole timer," James greeted him.

"Boy, what are you two doing here? I told you to take Meg to the picture show. Didn't you have enough money? I hear that restaurant I sent you too ain't cheap."

"We had enough money," James said. "We just decided to visit with you again. Here's your change."

"Keep it, boy. Keep it. Meg must have had a good time 'cause she don't look so uptight now. Now you give her plenty of time off and see that she relaxes some. After puttin' up with those high school kids all school year, she needs some downtime."

"My students aren't that bad," Meg said. "Most of them are pretty good kids. James isn't working me too hard either. The other day he took me to clean out the river, and we had a good time doing it." She looked at James and gently smiled.

"Do I sense a little romance in the air?" the older man asked.

James didn't say a word, so Meg spoke up. "No romance. You know, Bert, I'll never ... oh, forget it ... there are better things to talk about."

Meg didn't see James staring at her. He could easily see that with one simple question, the tense Meg was back.

On the way home, James tried several times to start a conversation, but Meg gave only monosyllabic answers. He eventually gave up trying to talk with her and drove in silence, wondering why Bert's question had caused her change in attitude. The soft music coming from the radio played on causing Meg to drift off to sleep.

When she began to lean toward James, he gently put his arm around her and drew her near enough to allow her head to rest in the hollow of his shoulder. She didn't see his contented smile as he hummed to the music. Meg snuggled in the comfort she found without even realizing she was doing it.

When they got back to the resort, James tapped the end of her nose. "Wake up ... we're home."

Before she was fully awake James pulled her into his arms and kissed her, first gently and then more urgently as she responded. After a very enjoyable minute, he released her.

"Now tell me," he challenged softly, "that there's no romance in the air."

"I didn't want to kiss you," she said sleepily. "You took advantage of my tiredness."

"It didn't seem that way to me." he said as he smoothed her hair away from her face. "Don't forget that trail ride tomorrow. Now I'd better get you to your room before you go back to sleep and have to spend the night in the van alone."

Meg couldn't forget the kiss or the comfort of being in James' embrace. For a moment, she had forgotten to keep up her defense.

"God, why does life have to be so unfair?" she asked before she drifted off to sleep. With the question hammering at her heart, a tear slid down her cheek, even as she slept.

Meg tried to avoid James the next day but didn't succeed. He came in the general store, plopped in the wooden rocking chair, and asked, "Which ride do you want to go on—the one o'clock or three o'clock?"

"James, I don't think we should—"

"I didn't ask what you thought. I want just a simple answer—one or three o'clock?"

"Three."

"See you then. I've got to get some canoes to the gravel bar."

The chair kept rocking after James' departure. Meg stared at it and realized it was like his presence. It continued, even after he left.

The phone called her attention back to business.

"A party of four for camping," she repeated back to the customer. "What kind of camper do you have? Do you want hookups, or do you want to rough it with primitive camping? No, sir, we don't have tubs—only showers. I'm sure your wife will be satisfied. We keep them very clean."

The rest of the day was busy, and Meg forgot to watch the time. She didn't realize it was close to three o'clock until James came back to check on her.

"Aren't you going to put jeans on?" he asked. "Those shorts aren't too practical for horseback riding."

"Who's going to watch the store? Things have been busy today. Maybe I should stay here."

"I've already seen to that. I'll watch the desk while you get ready, and Sue will be here in time to take over before we leave. Hurry and get changed."

The trail ride was fun. Meg and James were last in the line of horses and worked hard at not laughing out-loud at the minor catastrophes of the inexperienced riders in front of them.

"We can't laugh," she said quietly.

"I know, but you do have to admit that some of these people look mighty funny trying to ride a horse when the horse does its own thing. Look at that!" he said softly as a horse lay down in the shallow creek with the inexperienced rider hanging on.

The ride ended without major mishaps. James had been an enjoyable riding companion and hadn't touched Meg except to help her dismount—she was glad of that. *Or am I?* she wondered.

Chapter Four

*T*HE SUN WAS beginning to rise as Meg leaned against the porch railing of her cabin. Four weeks at the resort had already passed and, for the most part, she was enjoying her summer. The promise of a beautiful day had enticed her out of bed. She had been too excited to sleep and had risen early to wait for Bill and Sherry to arrive.

Meg had been exceptionally close to her brother, Bill, during their childhood. Bill, only a year younger than Meg, had been her constant companion. They had played both with dolls and trucks, and it had not mattered to either of them which it was.

As teenagers, they had remained close. The sibling rivalry that plagued most households had managed to escape the Greens. Meg thought happily of an incident during her junior year in high school.

She had been lying on her bed, studying for first-semester finals, when Bill came into her room and plopped down beside her.

"Well, big sister, I passed my driver's test on the first try today.

How many times did it take you to pass it?" Bill knew, of course, that Meg had taken the test three times, but he couldn't resist the brotherly tease. Meg had thrown her pillow at him for his taunt, but then congratulated him. They chatted a long time about their driving skills before he left her so she could resume studying.

When she was really honest with herself, she admitted that it bothered her that she was no longer the most important girl in Bill's life. Three years ago, he had wiped tears from his eyes as he saw his lovely Sherry coming down the aisle in her gown of white. She was aglow as she held her father's arm, but her eyes were only for her future husband. Guests commented on the love clearly evident on Bill's face as he watched Sherry. Since that eventful day, Meg had not been able to spend a lot of time with Bill and Sherry.

After their brief honeymoon, they'd gone directly to seminary. Meg had pleaded with them to come to River's View for a few days this summer, and her persistence had won. Today, they would arrive, and her excitement had triumphed over sleep.

A noise above her brought her attention to the huge oak near her cabin. She could barely see as a squirrel scampered from limb to limb, stopped, listened, and jumped again. Birds were chirping their morning songs as if to awaken the entire camp. Only Meg had stirred from her cabin. The giant red ball slowly rising above the eastern horizon insisted that daylight would very soon brighten the sky.

She was glad she'd been too excited to sleep, for she would have missed so much as God awakened the day. The quietness calmed her excitement as she glanced around the campground but saw no one moving in the morning's dawn.

Today was going to be a day she would remember for a long time. She could feel it in her bones.

———

"Bill! Sherry!" Meg cried as she ran to them and gave them big hugs before they'd even reached the door of the general store.

"Hey, big sister, let us at least get in the door before you start with all the mushy stuff. Be careful you don't hurt my little wifey."

"I'm not going to hurt Sherry, you big oaf." Meg laughed and hugged Sherry again.

"Meg, be careful," Bill stated seriously.

"Bill, are you crazy? I can't hurt her with a hug."

The young couple gave each other knowing glances. "We weren't going to tell you like this, but … we're going to be parents."

Meg turned pale. She took a step back and stammered, "Oh, Bill … Bill … how … how could you?"

"Meg," Bill said gently, "we've been through this many times. You know we have opposite viewpoints."

Meg looked at Sherry. "Do you agree with Bill?"

"Of course I do, or we wouldn't be so excited. Now be happy for us—and for yourself that you're going to have a niece or nephew to spoil. Give me another hug, and tell me congratulations."

Meg did as she was told but her concern clearly had not vanished.

Bill shook his head almost imperceptibly at Sherry, so she wouldn't say anything else to Meg about the baby. He would talk later with his sister.

———

Over a lunch of spaghetti in the cafeteria, Bill questioned Meg about her summer thus far. Meg told him about Bert's accident and going to visit him in the hospital.

"Who's taking Bert's place?"

"James Carson."

"There's a James Carson that attends my seminary," Bill noted.

Meg nodded her head. "One and the same."

"I've had classes with him. Seems like a nice guy but can't say that I know much about him. I do remember him arguing with our Christian Ethics professor. He had a strong opinion and wouldn't back down. The prof was a bit irked at him."

"What was he so adamant about?"

"Let me think a second … seems like it had something to do with handicapped people being able to contribute more than society will let them. I sure hope I get to spend some time with him. Since he's a year ahead of me, he can tell me which professors to get and which to avoid."

Bill and James do not need to spend time together, Meg thought, *especially around me.*

"What kind of horses were those we saw along the way to the resort?" Sherry asked. "They looked a lot bigger than the others way out in the field."

"Those are our Belgians that pull the wagon for the hayride," Meg answered. "Aren't they beauts? Their names are Pete and Charlie—Charlie's a mare."

"Bill, can we go? I love hayrides."

"Hayrides are always on Thursday evenings," Meg told them. "You can have your choice of a dusk or dark ride. At dusk, you'll still be able to see the countryside—fields, wildflowers, and trees. When it's dark, though, the ride is more romantic and a bit mysterious since no one knows what's coming next."

"Which should we do?" Sherry asked Bill. "See everything or be smoochers in the hay?"

"Let's see where we're going. Maybe then we'll discover what attracts Meg to come here each summer."

Meg had gotten up to retrieve some apple pie when she saw James approaching Bill.

"Bill, how are you doing?" James greeted him. "Meg, why did you not tell me Bill was coming?" he asked, as Meg returned to the table with dessert. She ignored his question and seated herself.

Bill instantly detected the tension between Meg and James and wondered what was happening between the two of them. As soon as James excused himself, Bill turned to Meg, asking "How do you like working with James?"

Meg shrugged. "Okay."

"That's all? Just okay?"

"I miss Bert. I really like him—he reminds me of our gramps."

"I bet James could be sweet too, if you'd give him a chance."

"No!" she responded much too quickly.

Bill raised his eyebrows at her reaction, reading it as the defense mechanism it was. "Give him a chance, sis. He might be the Prince Charming you've been wanting."

"There will be no Prince Charming for me," she flatly stated.

"There could be, but you're too stubborn to let anyone have a chance."

Meg gave her brother a good-natured shove, but before she could say anything, James returned to the table with his food tray.

"Can I get in on this conversation?" James asked.

Bill grinned. "I was just telling Meg that she's stubborn when it comes to finding herself a man."

"Is she now?" James said with a grin. "That could provide interesting entertainment for a guy who was determined to win her affection."

Bill started to agree, but when he saw Meg's discomfort, he quickly changed the subject. "James, I'd like to ask you about one of the professors …."

As Bill and James discussed seminary classes, Meg relaxed and chatted with Sherry. By the time the four left the building, the cafeteria was empty.

"How would you two like to be the judges for our scavenger hunt?" Meg questioned her brother and Sherry.

"Sounds interesting," Sherry said. "I'm always ready for a new adventure! What do we do?"

"We'll give the kids lists of things to find all over the campground," Meg explained. "Then the winners get prizes ranging from snow cones to River's View T-shirts to the most coveted prize—the horseback ride."

Meg made arrangements to meet Bill and Sherry on the porch of the general store after they unpacked and had time to go to the river to swim. James walked with Meg toward the general store, where she would continue working during the afternoon.

"Is it true?" he asked.

"Is what true?"

"That you don't let a guy have a chance to get to know you."

Thinking he already knew the answer, she looked at him and grinned.

James laughed at her. Placing his arm around her waist, he whispered, "You've just met your match, sweetheart!"

He was still chuckling when Meg turned from him and walked toward the store. She was so flustered that she almost ran into two campers.

James was gathering canoes from the river's edge when he spotted Bill and Sherry gathering their things from their afternoon of swimming. He noticed Sherry seemed to have a small baby bump. He hoped to get a chance to speak with Bill about his sister. Maybe Bill could help him understand Meg, because she surely had him confused.

He got his opportunity as he headed toward the boat barn with the load of canoes.

"Hey, James, wait up!" Bill called out to him. "Meg said something about free firewood. Where do I find it?"

"Jump in the truck. I'm headed that direction now." James wasted no time in questioning Meg's brother. "Were you teasing Meg, or does she really try to avoid guys?"

"Do I detect a bit of interest in my sister?"

"You could say that."

The ride to the woodpile hadn't taken long. Bill continued talking about his sister. "Meg and I were very close during our growing-up years, but on developing a relationship, she doesn't share information. I've watched her over the years, though, and she'll date a guy a few times and then drop him."

"Why?"

James and Bill threw wood into the pickup bed.

"I don't know. It almost seems like she's afraid to get involved."

"Did some man break her heart, so now she'd rather be safe than sorry? You know the saying, 'Once burned, twice shy.'"

More chunks of wood landed in the truck.

"Not that I know of, and I think I would have known if that had happened."

"Hm-m-m, I've always liked a challenge. I'm going to see if I can't get her to change her mind about at least one guy."

"Good luck. I think you're going to need it, but if you can get to the root of her problem, she's a great gal—even if she is my sister. Do you think you've got a chance with her?"

They had gotten enough firewood for a few campfires, and headed toward Bill's camping site.

"I know she likes me, but she's doing everything she can to convince me otherwise."

"Well, as I said, good luck."

Bill and Sherry were great as judges for the scavenger hunt. Twenty-five soda tabs, ten aluminum cans, a round rock, a nut, a dead dragonfly, a forked stick, a 1963 penny, three pine cones, and a dried oak leaf. Several children found all the items on the list, so Bill and Sherry did as Meg had instructed and rolled their round rocks to see which one went the straightest—the straightest rolling rock's owner was the winner.

"The winner of the horseback ride is ... Kimberly Ross!" Meg announced with a dramatic flair.

The child jumped up and down with glee. "I did it! I did it! I get a free horseback ride!" She ran to her parents for a well-deserved hug and congratulations.

"Don't forget your ticket for the ride," her dad instructed.

Kimberly went back to Meg, received a hug from her also, and got her ticket.

After the other prizes were awarded, Meg said, "Okay, kids. You've all done well too. There are free snow cones for everyone who participated."

"They've had a good time," commented Bill.

"They always do," Meg said. Then she whispered, "It's a great way to get the campground cleaned from small litter too!"

When the children finished their snow cones, Bill, Sherry, and Meg each enjoyed a snow cone. Meg told them that every Monday, Bert would let children earn a free horseback ride by having them clean the campground of litter left from the weekend. "He thought it was good for the kids to earn something instead of always getting a handout from Mom and Dad," Meg explained. "Bert's philosophy is to help kids learn to help themselves."

<hr>

When James came into the general store the next morning, Meg was frowning.

"What's wrong?" he asked.

"I'm just concerned about Sherry. Bill came in and got tickets for a canoe float trip, and I don't think Sherry should be floating in a canoe. She's pregnant. You know things happen on the water that could be dangerous for her."

"I'd noticed she's showing a small baby bump, but she appears to be fit enough. I don't think it will hurt her. If anything, she'll relax, and that will be good for her and the baby."

"Sounds just like a man," Meg said disgustedly. "What if the canoe flips and sinks? It takes two experienced people to pull it out of the water. That could be dangerous at this early stage of her pregnancy. What if a water moccasin decides to drop from a limb into the canoe, and Sherry panics and falls out? What if she gets too much sun?"

James stopped her. "What if you are borrowing trouble? What if you let them have a good time and not worry about them all day? Bill's responsible, and I know he'll take care of Sherry."

"Men! None of you have the sense God gave a goose!"

"Look, I've never been married, so I'm not too knowledgeable about pregnancy," James admitted freely, "but I do see pregnant women doing all kinds of things, including canoeing."

"*Hmph!* A lot you know about it!" Meg snorted, clearly becoming downright angry.

"Didn't I just tell you I'm not an expert on pregnancy?"

Meg started to get tears in her eyes. "She could lose the baby…"

"Look, if you're that upset about them floating, we'll get a canoe and stay close to them so we can be there to help if anything goes wrong. If the canoe flips, I'll be there to help Bill, and Sherry won't have to lift a finger. But I still think they'll be fine, whether we're there are not."

Meg burst into a radiant smile and gave James a quick hug. "Oh, James, thank you. I know I'll feel better about them in a canoe if we're close by so we can rescue them if they need it."

It didn't dawn on Meg until several minutes later that she had just agreed to spend time with James again. *Oh, well. It'll be worth putting up with James so we can be close to Bill and Sherry,* she told herself. She had seen too many canoe floaters sink their canoes not to be concerned.

Hugging James had brought Meg a surprising feeling of protection—one she didn't understand or even acknowledge, but it was there just the same. With him near, she felt safe.

The morning proved a good time for a float. It was neither too hot nor too cold, so Meg wore her shorts and blouse over her swimsuit. When they had to walk the canoe through the shallows, tennis shoes protected her feet from the sharp rocks on the river bottom. She had learned several summers ago—after she'd gotten a nasty cut from a broken bottle—to never go floating without sneakers on her feet.

"Did you bring any sunscreen lotion?" James asked. "My neck feels like it's getting burned."

"It's in the plastic bag. Help yourself."

"Since you're just sitting and day dreaming while I paddle, could you get it for me, and give it a pitch?"

After James had covered his neck with the white lotion, he tossed the bottle back to Meg. "What are you thinking about?" he asked. "You're sure quiet today and look like you're a thousand miles away."

"I'll never tell. It's a lady's privilege to keep her thoughts to herself, you know." Meg would not let James know she enjoyed being with him more than anyone she'd ever dated. She wanted to have a longer lasting relationship with him. His question brought her back to the reality of her life. Such a relationship could never be for her and James. God knew her daydreams were in vain.

"Bill and Sherry have stopped on the gravel bar by the swimming hole," James said. "Looks like we're going for a swim.

Would you dig into your bag and bring that lotion you just put away? After we swim, I'll have you rub more of it on my neck."

Meg stepped out of the canoe onto the gravel bar and sat beside Bill and Sherry. When James joined them, all four began pulling off their sneakers to get the tiny rocks out of their shoes before they went swimming. Although floaters couldn't go without sneakers, tiny rocks were a continual problem when they went down the river.

"I can't get the little stuff off my feet," Meg complained as she got up to walk toward the water. "It sure would be nice if we had sandy beaches by rivers. Maybe I ought to go work on the ocean front next year. Then I could step on sand instead of rocks." She went into the water to wash the last of the small rocks off her feet. Unexpectedly, she stepped on a slimy rock, and down she went. "Oh-h-h!" she groaned as she got up and glanced at the three still sitting on the gravel bar, laughing at her.

"Meg, I think you and slimy rocks have an attraction to one another," James teased. "How do you manage to find them so often?" When she didn't respond, he added, "I would have rinsed your shoes for you if you'd asked."

"I can do it myself, thank you very much. Besides, it wasn't just my shoes that had rocks in them. My feet had them stuck to them too."

Meg went back to the gravel bar and sat between Bill and James.

James looked at her feet. "Your feet have gravel on them again."

Before she knew what was happening, he scooped her up and carried her toward a deeper part of the river.

"Put me down!" she demanded. "I'm going to scream. *What* are you doing?"

Water was splashing on both of them as James hurriedly carried her farther into the river.

"Don't you drop me! Do you hear me, James?" she screamed as she flung her arms around his neck. "So help me, if you drop me out here, you're going down with me."

"Just what I like," James said softly, "a woman with spunk and determination." With that said, he quickly pulled her arms loose from his neck and dropped her into the water. He left her sputtering and splashing to gain her balance as he walked back to the gravel bar. "Your feet don't have rocks on them anymore!" he shouted back to her.

"James Carson, you're going to pay for this!" Meg hollered, her eyes bright with anger. She clenched her teeth and muttered, "You are the most despicable man I've ever had the misfortune to meet."

As James rejoined Bill and Sherry, he said, "I think Meg's ready to move on. Let's go." He headed toward the canoe, where the angry Meg had seated herself.

Bill and Sherry had not even gotten to swim.

Bill patted James on the back. "Well done, buddy. I think my sister's met her match."

Shortly after they'd pushed off, James said to Meg, "You didn't put lotion on my neck."

"Do it yourself!" she insisted but got the lotion out of the bag. She sighed exasperatedly and said, "Turn around if you want me to do it," Meg said as she moved closer to him in the canoe. She considered squeezing the whole tube on top of his head but wasn't quite brave enough to risk the repercussions she knew it would bring. Instead, she roughly slapped some on his neck and rubbed as hard as she could.

"Hey, take it easy. It's starting to get sore."

"Too bad. It serves you right for dropping me in the water." Gradually, however, she eased up until she was gently massaging the white lotion into his skin. She rubbed a little longer than necessary, until her touch became a gentle caress.

"Nice touch you have there," he quietly said as he turned to look her in the eye. But before he could see the look he hoped to see, she quickly turned her head away and moved back to her seat.

"You'd better pay attention to where this canoe's going," Meg instructed him, "or we're going to land under that fallen tree."

James grabbed his paddle and added, "Well, get your paddle and start working too. You're not in this for a free canoe ride, you know."

Meg ignored his rebuke. "I wouldn't want to hurt your

masculinity by helping you paddle. You're doing a fine job. I think I'll lie over the seat and ice chest and dry out from my unplanned swim." And she did just that.

Smiling down at her, he watched as she closed her eyes and covered them with her arm. He began to hum one song after another as he expertly paddled.

"If you're going to keep me awake, you could at least sing to me instead of humming." She had turned her head and looked at him with green eyes that he could not resist.

Without comment, he began to sing everything he could think of, from the most popular country-western songs to his favorite hymns and praise songs. For almost half an hour, they drifted along.

Bill and Sherry were always within sight, as James had promised they'd be, yet it seemed to James and Meg that they were alone. When at last she sat up, he stopped singing.

"You're quite good," Meg told him. "Do you ever sing publicly?"

"Sometimes, but I'd rather speak or preach. Mostly I like to sing for my own enjoyment. When I get to feeling low in spirits, singing helps to lift my mood."

"Are you not enjoying yourself today?"

"I didn't say that was the *only* time I liked to sing. Sometimes I do it just for the pleasure it brings, and today was one of those times. Besides, I think there is someone in the boat with me who liked it." He flashed a grin at her but then admitted, "Okay, I have been a little down."

"Can I ask you something?"

James nodded agreeably as he continued to paddle. "Sure, ask away."

"Do you struggle with your faith, or does it come easy for you?"

"Some of both, I guess. How about you?" James asked.

"I'm like you. Sometimes I have great faith and don't question God, but other times, I wonder if He's really working everything for my good. When things get tough, I start questioning His wisdom."

"Are you referring to anything specific?" he asked. "Maybe I can help."

"Oh, nothing in particular," she lied. There was no way she was going to tell him how much she wanted their friendship to grow into a lasting relationship. And she certainly couldn't tell him why she never would allow it to do so.

By the time lunch rolled around, the four canoe floaters had worked up an appetite. Ahead of James and Meg, Bill and Sherry found a rocky island and waved to his sister and James to join them. Bill was already unloading the ice chest when James and Meg pulled ashore, and Sherry was spreading a cloth over the rocks.

"Did you have that chest tied to the canoe?" James asked.

"Were we supposed to?" Bill asked.

James grinned. "Only if you want to ensure that you keep it. Floaters are notorious for turning their canoes over—especially inexperienced folks like you. When you flip a canoe, everything happens so fast, you don't have time to grab your stuff before it sinks. It's tough going to pull heavier things like ice chests out of the water. I've got some extra rope so when we leave, you can tie it down. I don't want you to lose it."

As they gathered together for lunch, Meg wondered why any food taken on a float trip tasted so much better than it did at home. She was eager to see what Ginger had packed for them.

"You gals can get our lunch ready," Bill said. "James and I have been paddling all morning while you two sat on the canoes like princesses." With that, Bill and James sat down on the cloth, while Sherry and Meg pulled out fried chicken, potato salad, deviled eggs, and cold baked beans. The four of them ate with gusto, and then they all lay back to relax before continuing the float.

"It's not normal to have a tablecloth along the river," James commented dryly.

"That's just the way Sherry is," Bill responded. "Things are so neat and pretty at our house Sherry doesn't even keep a junk drawer."

"Do you want me to change my ways?" Sherry questioned, her eyes still closed to the glaring sun.

"Well, it would be nice if you didn't wipe the ring left by my coffee cup before I finish my coffee."

"Stop picking on her," Meg defended her sister-in-law. "She's the best thing that ever happened to you. You adore her, and you know it."

"Quiet, Meg," Bill responded. "If she knows that, she'll stop spoiling me, and I like it." He looked toward his wife, still contentedly lying on the gravel bar. The conversation had not disturbed her, because she knew she was loved by a man who delighted in teasing her.

"Are you guys trying to set an example of wedded bliss for Meg and me?" James asked.

"Maybe for you, but not for me," Meg replied.

James wouldn't leave the subject alone. "Meg, you don't seem the type to stay single. You have so much love to give. I see how you care for people and interact with the kids around the resort. You have a lot going for you that guys like—and that includes me. You're fun and very attractive too. Why do you say you don't want to marry? Are you just playing hard to get?" James had thrown down the gauntlet and now waited to see if Meg would pick it up.

"Thanks for the compliments," Meg said, although she was taken aback by James' words. "I'm not playing hard to get. That's just the way it is. I don't want to discuss the subject." She quickly looked directly at the river. She didn't want the other three to see the tears that had unexplainably come to her eyes. She had struggled with the decision to remain single, made up her mind, and now she was sticking with it no matter how hard it was. James' comments, however, made her question whether she had made the right choice.

Although James couldn't see her eyes, he guessed why Meg had turned suddenly to stare at the river. It was the reaction he had wanted to see. He now knew for certain that she was not as determined to stay single as she pretended to be. He sat silently, beginning to carefully set his strategy to break through the wall Meg had firmly erected around her heart. There had to be a weak spot in that wall, and he was determined he'd find it and get through to her. It might take a while, but he was a patient man—a very patient man.

James began talking to Bill about a sports team close to the seminary. Sherry occasionally joined the discussion, but Meg knew nothing about it and felt totally left out.

The smell of the fried chicken continued to float through the air. "Meg, would you hand me another piece of chicken?" James asked. "It smells too good to ignore it any longer."

"Hold on. I'll get it in a minute." She gave his hand a pat, as if reassuring a child that patience would eventually win the day.

He put his hand on hers, and as he did, sparks flew up her arm. Their eyes met, and she read the look in his eyes that said he liked her a lot. Her lips tightened as she reached for the piece of chicken and handed it to him.

He leaned toward her and said quietly, "I will win, you know."

"You are the most conceited male I have ever known in my life," she hissed back.

"And you're the most stubborn female I've ever met! Don't try to pretend you're immune to me, Meg. You like me, but don't expect God to send you a personal telegram from heaven to tell you it's okay to do so. He gave you feelings and reasoning, but you won't accept them. You're too afraid you might get to know me and like me. And you're afraid I will get to know and love the real Monica Elizabeth Green, not the carefree Meg who pretends she doesn't care about me. I can guarantee you, however, that I'm not interested in the act you seem to delight in playing."

"I'm not acting. I'm just afraid---"

James tossed his uneaten piece of chicken in the river, stood and turned his back as he walked farther up the gravel bar, leaving the three of them sitting there. Meg could feel his anger as he walked away without speaking.

Bill and Sherry looked at James, then back at Meg, and finally at one another. Bill raised his eyebrows at Sherry, who raised her finger to her lips. Sometimes silence truly was golden and needed to be allowed to exist.

After a few minutes, Meg spoke. "James had no right to say that to me. I've told him from the first time he asked me out that

I was not going to get serious about any guy. How dare he accuse me of acting!"

Bill and Sherry still sat silently, surprised to hear the outbursts from both James and Meg. It was evident Meg was fuming as much as James. He'd walked away to keep from causing a scene, and she was smarting from his rebuke. Bill and Sherry began conversation again, but Meg didn't hear them. She wondered if James had a point. Was she afraid of her feelings? Was she "acting"? Did she care about James more than she admitted, even to herself?

That's a dumb thought, she told herself. *I'm crazy about the guy, and I know it. I just can't let him know it.* She knew she was going to have to be on guard constantly around him.

Bill decided it was time to lighten the mood before the two of them got in a real argument. "Meg, let's get in the water for a bit." Then he hollered loud enough for James to hear. "We're getting in the water! Come join us."

"We're not supposed to swim after we eat," Meg recited dryly.

"You're right. But if you will notice, the water's only about four feet deep here. The chance of our drowning is minute."

James joined them but still had a scowl on his face, one that identically matched Meg's.

"What's wrong with you two?" Bill asked. "The tension between you is thick enough to cut."

Sherry wanted a word on the subject too. "James, I think you need to pay a little more attention to Meg. We women like to be babied a bit."

His scowl disappeared as he replied, "Okay, little mama-to-be, just for you, I'll pay attention to her." With that he grabbed Meg's hand and pulled her toward him. "Come on, Meg. We're ruining their day with our fussing. Let's get in the water for a bit."

Meg refused to even look at James, let alone respond, and her feet didn't move.

"That's it," he stated flatly. "We're getting packed up and going back to the resort. I've been watching Bill. He can handle that canoe okay, but we're not handling our emotions so well. There's no reason to ruin their day."

Still Meg didn't say a word, but she did as he had ordered. She gathered the lunch remains they had brought and stashed them in the canoe. James told the other couple they would leave them in peace to enjoy their day. He politely excused himself and Meg as he rowed away from them. He didn't even remember to give Bill a rope to tie around the ice chest.

Bill and Sherry stared after the sparring couple. Bill spoke first, "Whew, James has got his work cut out for him with my sister. She's stubborn as that mule we saw over with the horses. Do you want to know what's weird?"

Sherry acknowledged she did, and Bill said, "I can tell she really likes James. I think the battle is between her and God, and not her and James. She has not recognized that God is sovereign, and He alone determines the future. Until she overcomes the spiritual battle, she is going to be miserable and make James' existence really rough."

Sherry wasn't sure what Bill meant and decided she'd ask him about it sometime, but not now. She just wanted to enjoy her vacation time with her husband.

James and Meg reached a spot where they could get out of the water and quickly get back to the resort. Instead of James sounding angry, as Meg feared he would, he just looked at her with love in his eyes and smiled. He pulled her to him, wrapped his arms around her, and gave her a gentle kiss she did not resist. Then he held her away from him.

"Don't fret, Meg. We'll work things out."

She returned his smile. "Are you sure?"

"I'm sure. Now, I've got some things that I need to handle here at the resort. You take the rest of the day off. Maybe I'll see you at supper."

Meg stared in confusion at his retreating figure. She had expected a big argument, but he just walked away, leaving her confused, bewildered, and very alone. He had not attempted to convince her that her attitude was wrong.

Chapter Five

*A*T SUPPER THAT evening, Bill asked Meg if she would go on the hayride with him and Sherry. Now, dressed in her jeans and a long-sleeve plaid shirt, she stood talking with them when she saw the hay wagon approaching. The big Belgians, Pete and Charlie, were such beautiful horses that Meg never tired of admiring their beauty and strength. Staring at the horses, she had not noticed that James was the driver of the team until he spoke, "Hey, Meg. If I had known you wanted to go on the hayride, I would have sat in the back with you. But I volunteered to drive for Mack tonight. Come up here on the seat and ride with me." He patted the spot where he wanted her to sit as she reluctantly climbed aboard.

"Bill, did you arrange this?" Sherry whispered to her husband.

Bill's eyes seemed to answer his wife's question. "It seems to me our friend James needs a little assistance with my hard-headed sister. I just happened to mention to him that she was going on the hayride with us."

"All right, Cupid. Now you'll have to keep me happy all by yourself."

"That would be my pleasure, Mrs. Green." Bill pulled her close to him. "Come on. Let's get a seat as far away from my matchmaking as possible. I don't want to hear the reaction if James lets it slip that I told him Meg was coming on the hayride."

On the front seat, Meg looked at James. "I think I should go sit by Bill and Sherry since they invited me to come along."

"Suit yourself, if there's enough space for you back there."

She turned to look at the back of the wagon and saw it was full. "Too late. Guess I'll have to stay here with you. Oh, well, I've never ridden on the seat before. Are you a good teamster?"

"You're going to have to judge that for yourself, but I've driven Pete and Charlie lots of times, if that gives you any assurance. I think they know the route by heart now. If things get rough, I'll handle them with one arm and hold you with the other."

"Forget that! I know enough about these horses to know it takes two hands to control them. You drive. I'll ride and do my best not to fall off the seat or get hit by a low-hanging branch."

Noticing everyone was onboard, James popped the reins. Pete and Charlie began a slow walk through the campground. Meg saw the campers beginning to make their campfires for the evening, children playing, and a few finishing up their evening meal.

Some had already put their chairs around the campfires. The smoky fires permeated the atmosphere. Meg breathed in deeply, enjoying the woodsy fragrance. Life was simple and relaxing in the campground—no students, no papers to grade, no rush. Tonight, she decided, she would relax and enjoy the ride, sitting beside James.

She smiled at him, and he grinned back. "So far, so good?" he asked.

"Yep, I love it here at the resort. There's no place like it for me. I wish I could live here year-round."

"What about your students? You said you like teaching."

"I do, but this place is so relaxing, I'd give up teaching if I could live here all the time."

"I know what you mean, but I worked here during my last year of high school. It's not much fun in the winter. The river's frozen, the horses have to have special care, storms blow limbs down ... firewood to cut ... it's just work in the winter ... no relaxation."

After riding through the campground area, the wagon trail began to wind through the fields. The fragrance of wildflowers and hay waiting to be baled drifted back to her. She eyed James' arms and saw his muscles constrict and expand as he expertly guided the big horses. Without warning, he raised a rein and smacked Pete on the flank. The startled horse took off faster, forcing Charlie to keep up with him. Just as suddenly, James slowed them down to a walk.

"Why did you do that?" Meg demanded. "I can't stand cruelty to animals. I expected better of you!"

"Would you prefer I let the bee that had landed on him sting and then startle him? There would be no stopping him then."

"Sorry. I didn't see the bee. Did you get it off Pete?"

"Do you see it now? I wouldn't be cruel to an animal. I'd think you know me well enough by now to be ashamed of yourself for even suggesting it."

The riders in the wagon, oblivious to the conversation or the bee, had enjoyed the quick burst of speed from the horses.

"You do get irritated at me sometimes," Meg said. "I thought you were mad at the horse like you get aggravated with me."

"You can make me madder than anyone I know. I like you a lot, and you do your best to make me mad. One of these days, you just might win this war. Then you can be an old maid school teacher in Alaska, and I can find someone who appreciates me!"

"I appreciate the work you do here. You've been a godsend for Bert this summer."

"That's not the appreciation I'm talking about, and you know it. You are too stubborn for your own good. What's the bee in your bonnet that makes you so stinkin' independent?"

"Drop it, James. I want to enjoy the ride."

Here she goes again, James thought. *She's avoiding the issue. I am going to find out what her problem is if it's the last thing I do.* With that thought in mind, he reached around Meg, took her hands, and placed the reins in them.

Startled, she asked, "What are you doing? I can't handle these horses!"

With his fingers continuing to place the reins properly in her hands, James arms stayed around her. She relaxed against him and let him instruct her. "I'm right here beside you. Just trust me. Okay, pull them a bit to the right."

Under James' tutelage, she drove the team of massive Belgians as they walked the trail.

In a couple of minutes, James took the reins back. "It wasn't so hard to trust me for a minute, was it? Trust is hard, Meg. Work at learning to do it."

With a sharp snap of the reins and a "giddy-up" from James, the horses took off running. The riders screamed as they bolted through a creek, and water splashed everywhere. As soon as they were out of the creek bed, he slowed the team down again.

He whispered conspiratorially, "We have to give them a few thrills, so they'll want to ride again. Hang on—there's another spot coming up."

Her smile was spontaneous as she shared his enthusiasm for the thrill he was providing not only the riders, but her as well. Her green eyes danced with delight when she looked at him.

Again, he snapped the reins, and the horses bolted through a depression in the trail.

"Mr. Carson, that's lots of fun," a child's voice yelled from the wagon. "Do it again! Do it again!"

He did his best to accommodate the child at each dip in the trail. Meg's pleasure with the ride as she sat beside him made him even more determined to unravel the mystery behind her reluctance to let him get close to her. He knew he would eventually learn the reason. Somehow, he knew the problem went deeper than playing hard to get. Why would she not let him—or for that matter, any man—get close to her? *Monica Elizabeth Green*, he thought, *you won't find this man quite so easy to throw away. I believe you're the woman God wants for me, and I'm willing to work on this puzzle until it's solved.*

Meg had to duck to keep from being hit by a low-hanging branch. As she raised back up, she looked at him. "What are you smiling about? Do you want me to get knocked off the seat?"

"My thoughts didn't have anything to do with your getting knocked off the seat."

He brought the wagon back toward the loading area. "I don't think you want to know what I was thinking."

"Thinking you want to knock me unconscious with that branch, I bet. Then I'd be out of your hair for a while."

"Okay, you asked for my thoughts, so here goes. I was thinking I want to get better acquainted with a beautiful lady I know. In fact, I think she might end up being my wife."

"Oh, is she someone I know?"

"I'll never tell. How about going on the dusk ride with me too?"

"No, thanks. This is Bill and Sherry's last night, and I want to spend my time with them."

In bed that night, Meg couldn't sleep. She was plagued by jealousy. Who was the beautiful lady James had mentioned? The longer she thought about it, the more disturbed she became. How dare he be with her and think about someone else! With a frown on her face, she eventually drifted into an uneasy sleep. She dreamed of James at his wedding, smiling at the beautiful girl by his side, while she stood off at a distance, crying. It was too late to tell him she loved him.

―――――――

"Meg … are you in there?"

Meg recognized Sherry's voice coming through her door.

Rising from her bed, Meg saw the sun was already brightly shining. Her restless night had caused her to sleep late. "I'm here. Come on in. Looks like I overslept."

Sherry spoke to her sister-in-law as she entered, "We wondered at breakfast what happened to you. Bill and I are getting ready to leave in a few minutes but didn't want to go without saying good-bye."

"Don't leave without letting me give you both hugs. Give me just five minutes, and I'll meet you in the parking lot."

Meg quickly dressed and rushed to get her hugs and say good-bye. As she approached, she saw Bill and James talking. James had one booted foot propped on the wooden fence rail. Clean jeans and a new western shirt made him look more ruggedly handsome than ever.

"It's about time you got up, sleepyhead." Bill tousled the hair she'd just run a brush through. He'd been tousling her hair since his height overcame hers by several inches, and she wasn't tall or strong enough do anything about it. She pushed it back in place without a comment.

Sherry gave Meg a squeeze. "We didn't want to leave without saying bye to you. These guys are talking serious stuff."

"We were just talking about you, big sister."

"Me? Why were you talking about me?"

"Don't tell her, Bill," James insisted. "Let's keep her guessing."

"Hey, you guys aren't playing fair." Meg looked from James to Bill but got no answer.

"Come on, Sherry," Bill said. "Let's get out of here before James and I get in trouble with my sister. She was nice enough to provide us a few days of vacation, and we might want her to do the same next year."

Meg and James watched as the car spit dust off the gravel road.

"Thanks for inviting them to come this summer. I didn't know Bill very well, but it was a great opportunity to get better acquainted with my future brother-in-law."

"When pigs fly!" Meg's response was so quick, she caught James off guard. He threw his head back and laughed as he walked away. *That man does not plan to leave the subject alone,* she thought. Her temper cooled as fast as it had sparked. *If only it could be true,* she wished. Meg looked at her watch. If she didn't hurry, she'd be late for work. She rushed through the parking lot, up the steps, and unlocked the door just as the first customer of the day joined her.

Back in the general store, Meg expected to see James come in to pester her, but he didn't. Each time the door opened, she glanced up, ready to tell him exactly what she thought of his plan to marry her. Each time, she had to swallow what she wanted to say as guests came for one reason or another. After taking time off while Bill and Sherry were here, she had some catching up to do and settled down to complete her work journals.

When finally he did come in, she immediately knew something had upset him. He looked like he'd been crying. Before she could speak, he said, "I've got to go home immediately, so I'm leaving you in charge. Take care of the resort for Bert as if it was your own property. I'll be back in three days."

"What's wrong? I can tell something's got you upset."

He lightly stroked her cheek with his finger. "Not now, little one. I'll tell you about it when I get back. Look after things here for me."

There was sadness about him she had not seen since she'd met him. He gathered her to him, looked deeply into her eyes, and brushed his lips against hers. The next thing she knew, he was out the door.

He was gone, and she hadn't gotten to tell him what she thought of his marriage plan. Now she wasn't sure she wanted to tell him. She felt vulnerable and alone. She began talking aloud to herself—something she did only when she was upset.

———

"Who are you talking to, Meg?"

"Hi, Chuck. Just talking to myself. I was getting ready to tell James what I think of some of his assumptions, but he walked out before I could tell him."

"He's a pretty decent sort of guy, but it seems to me your timing was a little off."

"What do you mean?"

"Didn't you know? He just got a phone call from home. His little sister died—the one that was severely handicapped."

Meg's mouth dropped open in surprise. "But he didn't say a word about her. Just a few days ago, he told me she was doing well.

All he said was that I was in charge until he got back. I feel bad that I didn't know." Meg said.

"Look, he didn't tell you—you just told me that yourself. I'm sure he had a reason for not sharing. I wouldn't have known either, except I was with him when he got the call. He was pretty upset, let me tell you."

Tears rolled down Meg's cheeks.

"Hey, come on, Meg. I don't know what to do when a woman cries. Stop." She did the opposite as sobs racked her body. Fortunately no customers were in the store.

When she began to shake, Chuck patted her back and spoke to her in soft tones to try to calm her down. "You may be a teacher, and I'm just a kid, but it looks to me like you care for James, or you wouldn't be so upset at this situation and yourself. Am I right?"

Meg nodded her head. When Meg didn't stop crying, Chuck decided he needed to take action. He put the "temporarily closed" sign on the general store door without asking her if it was okay to do so.

"Go wash your face and freshen yourself up a bit," Chuck instructed. "James is counting on you."

Meg went to the rest room, splashed her face with cold water, and took several deep breaths before returning to Chuck. She was beginning get herself under control.

Chuck kept silent as Meg continued to regain her composure.

"Is it safe to take the sign down yet? There are several people on the porch waiting to come inside."

When Meg nodded, he opened the door and welcomed the guests. Meg was immediately thrust into the role of supervisor of River's View Resort.

Meg was pleased that things ran smoothly at the campground for the remainder of the day. She prayed for James as she worked, asking God to comfort his heart but wondering why he had not shared with her that his sister had died.

After counting the day's receipts, which James did each evening, she walked through the park to make sure everything was all right with the campers. She stopped to visit with a young family who were busy setting up their tent. "Good evening, folks," she said. "I'm the acting manager for the evening. Is there anything I can do for you?"

"You could hold the baby for a minute so I can help my husband get the tent in place. My name's Karen Davenport, and this is my husband, Greg."

"I remember you registering this afternoon," Meg said as she reached to take the baby. "I'm afraid I didn't remember your names though. What's the baby's name?"

"Jennifer," Karen answered as she began helping her husband. "This is our first camping trip since she was born. We're sure hoping Jenny does okay away from her bed."

"We get a lot of children here at the resort and very few have problems. So far, she seems content enough." The baby grabbed a handful of Meg's hair and smiled a toothless grin at her. "Turn loose, sweetie," Meg pleaded.

"I'm afraid you'll have to pry her fingers loose. She's just discovered hair and thinks it's the neatest thing going. If it keeps up, I might decide to get mine cut," the baby's mother injected.

With the tent set up and bedding in place, they thanked Meg as she left them to visit with other campers before heading to her cabin for the evening. Glancing toward the sky, she saw lightning in the distance. She had heard the forecast but hoped it wouldn't rain. Rain made such a mess of the campgrounds and created irritable campers, as their bedding and food supplies got wet.

Preparing for bed, she wondered again why James had not told her about his sister. She thought of the time they'd spent together over the past few weeks. Even though a lot of it was work related, she hoped he knew she was concerned about him. But how could he know that she cared? Over and over, she had rebuffed his overtures of friendship and had refused to let it grow. He wanted more of their relationship than she was willing to give. She also knew she had come to rely on him a lot more than she was saying to others.

As she listened to the thunder coming closer to the resort, Meg wished James was near. What would she do if the electricity went out or lightning struck a tree and fell on someone's tent before they could seek refuge from the storm? Even worse, what if there was a flash flood and many people drowned?

Meg gave herself a mental scolding. *Pull yourself together and stop thinking like that. You're borrowing trouble again.*

She began to pray for protection for the campers and herself. She knew she could tell God exactly how she was feeling. "God, I'm scared. You know storms frighten me, and I don't have anyone to help me if something happens." Then her prayer wandered to a different direction. "I want James here to hold me. I want to trust him, but you know why I can't. Why can't I get married and have a loving husband like my friends? God, I don't want to stay single, but I can't get married. You're the one that made it impossible for me. Why did you do it? Why, why, why?"

Meg was so engrossed with raging at God that she forgot about the storm until a loud clap of thunder brought her attention back to the situation at hand. "Oh, God, I'm sorry. I'm so weak, but I'm trying to trust you. Please don't let me be afraid. Help me get through these days until James gets back."

Thunder, lightning, and rain continued to blast the campground for two hours but eventually rolled to the distance, leaving a soaked campground and an exhausted Meg, sound asleep. It was hard work to fear the unknown.

At breakfast the next morning, the thunderstorm was the topic of staff conversations. Meg admitted storms frightened her, and she was teased by Chuck and Tony, another of the high school summer workers.

"I can't believe a teacher's afraid of a little storm," Chuck scoffed. "C'mon, Meg, you're tougher than that."

"I am tough in the classroom, but I get really scared in storms. I turn into a frightened child again."

"What you needed last night was James." At Meg's scoff, Chuck decided it was time to get out of there. "I think I'd better get to work."

Mattie stared at her. "You've been moody this summer. Is James the reason you're not your usually feisty self?" Seeing Meg's downcast look, Mattie said, "Hey, forget I asked, okay? You just showed me the answer to my question. If you want to talk about him, you know I've got a good listening ear. Anytime you want to come over to the snack shack, sit on the stool, and talk, you just come right ahead. That stool and I make good counselors."

―――――――

Later that day Meg became concerned about a group of young men who had checked in for two nights. She wanted them to have a good time, but they had smelled of liquor when they arrived. She emphasized to them that the campground quiet hours began at 10 p.m. and drunkenness was not permitted.

"Yes, ma'am, pretty lady. If you come over to my tent about 10:05, you can ensure a nice night in my tent. It might not be too quiet though," he said, laughing obnoxiously. He leaned toward Meg in an attempt to get closer to her, but she stepped backward to avoid his odor. "What's wrong, babe? Don't you like me?"

"Leave her alone, Jerry," his buddy said. "Can't you tell she's not your type?"

Meg heard nothing further from the group, but Jerry's curses as he left the general store rang in her ears.

After supper, Meg and Mattie took two of the horses and made the evening tour of the grounds. Walking the horses was faster than going by foot, and the women enjoyed their ride and talk with one another.

Mattie decided it was time to talk to Meg about James. "I don't think you're being fair to James. This morning you were almost in tears when I mentioned his name, yet you won't give the guy a chance. I've seen the way he looks at you. He adores you. Why don't you encourage him a little instead of being so cold to him? He seems like a super nice guy to me."

Mattie seemed ready to continue, but Meg stopped her. "I don't think I'm cold to him at all. We've gone out several times. I'm just not interested in romance. I'll be glad when this summer's over, and I never have to lay eyes on James Carson again."

"For once, think with your heart, not your brain. Why do you think James put you in the general store? Isn't his office in a room there? Why do you think he asked you to clean the river with him?"

"I'm in the store because that's where I've always worked."

"What about the river cleanup? Was that all work? Were the horseback and wagon rides nothing but work?" Mattie continued to try to reason with Meg. "I can see I'm wasting my breath talking to you. James is a good guy, and you could be a real asset to his ministry—whatever he decides to do—but I don't think you'll even consider it. You've told me to pray about things in the past. Why don't you at least pray about your relationship with James? Maybe God can change that stubborn streak you've got. Sure as shootin', nobody else can faze it." Mattie dug her heels into the horse's side and took off for the stables, leaving a chastised Meg staring at her back.

———

"Stop banging on your desk!" Meg said but hadn't yet fully awakened.

"Meg, wake up!" came the voice through her door as the banging continued. Meg was a sound sleeper and mumbled again, "I said to stop banging on your desk."

"It's me, Chuck. You're not at school. You're dreaming. Now wake up--there's a problem in the campground."

Finally awake, Meg shuffled to the door. "What's wrong?"

"There's trouble in the campground. I met a guy, mad as a hornet, who was trying to find the manager. Those guys that came in today are drinking and causing a lot of disturbance, and no one is getting any sleep. If we don't get them quieted down, we're going to lose some customers."

Meg told Chuck to wait for her and then pulled on jeans and a T-shirt. She ran her fingers through her hair, as she opened the door and instructed Chuck, "Go call the sheriff. They were told the rules, so they'll have to be thrown out. You know Bert doesn't put up with drunks. I'm heading down there to see if I can quiet them down."

"I don't think you should go by yourself."

"I'll be fine. Now go call the sheriff. The sooner those guys leave, the better off we'll be."

Meg wasn't nearly as confident of her ability to quiet the guys as she pretended to be with Chuck. She'd never had to face troublesome guests before, and she was frightened. She hoped her "teacher voice" would do the trick and get them to leave before the sheriff arrived.

Before she could see the campsite, she could hear their boisterous noise. Loud music and liquor had enlivened the men. She threw her shoulders back as she approached them and said in her toughest school teacher voice, "Men, I'm going to have to ask you to leave the resort. We're getting complaints about your noise. You were told quiet was expected after 10 p.m. You're keeping everyone awake around you."

The men acted as if they hadn't heard her. The loudest one, Jerry, approached her. The alcohol on his breath made her flinch, but she didn't back away. "If it ain't the pretty lady from the store. Glad you came to join us." He took her arm and began pulling her toward the others. "Hey, fellas, pretty lady, here is gonna join our little party."

"You're not listening," Meg said sternly, looking directly at him as she spoke. "I said you must leave the resort."

He pulled her to a log the men had rolled up to sit on and laughed at her as he pushed her down. "Who's gonna make us? Sure ain't gonna be you." Jerry tried to sit beside her but slid off the log.

She tried again. "Men, I'm asking you to quietly pack your things and leave—*now!*"

"Pretty lady, I like you," Jerry slurred in his drunken state. "Come on, let's have some fun." He began pulling Meg toward his pup tent.

"Let go of me—you're drunk!"

"Yep, I reckon I'm drunk, but I ain't too drunk to show you a good time." As he pushed her toward the tent flap, Meg panicked and fell to the ground. She tried to get to her feet, but the big drunk plopped on top of her.

"Come on, babe. Loosen up. I just want to show you a good time."

"Get off me!" she screamed. He tried to kiss her, and she screamed again. "Help! Someone help me!"

Jerry cursed violently and rolled off her. "Ain't you never had no fun before? I ain't gonna hurt you."

Headlights shone on the campsite as the sheriff came around the bend of the road. She could hear Chuck talking fast and loud. "Meg's here somewhere, Sheriff. At least she said she was coming here."

"Sheriff? You stupid fool. Why didn't you tell me you'd called the cops?" Jerry stood and attempted to walk. He stumbled and landed on his tent, knocking it flat.

Meg stood up and tried to regain her composure but could already feel the bruises forming on her lips and back from Jerry's plopping on her.

Chuck ran to her as the sheriff took charge. "Did that guy hurt you?" Chuck asked. "I'll beat him to a pulp."

His teenage protectiveness warmed Meg's heart. "I'm okay," she assured him, "just a bit shaken. Jerry's drunk, but he scared me half to death. I fell, and he plopped down on top of me. I imagine I'm going to have a few bruises tomorrow. He probably weighs 250 pounds." She tried to smile for Chuck's sake but burst out crying instead.

He put his arm around her shoulders and held her until the tears were gone.

When the sheriff told the guys they were sleeping it off in his jail, they cussed loud and long. "We ain't done nothin', Sheriff. Just havin' fun. All we've had is a few beers."

When the last man was loaded in the squad car, Chuck walked toward the sheriff and thanked him for coming. Meg heard Chuck tell him, "Just wait 'til James hears about this. He's not going to be happy." Then Chuck offered to walk Meg to her cabin. She was glad to have his company across the campground which had little light. Other guests were settling into their tents after scrambling from them to see the commotion. The grounds would be getting quiet again as soon as everyone settled down.

When she looked in the mirror the next morning, it was just as she'd expected. Her upper lip was bruised and swollen. Her eyes were red from crying, and her head ached from the stress of the night before. Stretching, she discovered her back was sore too. She would be so glad to see James, so he could take over as manager again. She hated the job.

All the workers questioned her as she ate breakfast. As soon as their curiosity was satisfied, she retreated to James' office. She wanted the records up-to-date before he got back. She was so absorbed in her task that she didn't hear James come in.

"What in the world did you think you were doing by trying to throw those guys out on your own last night? Don't you know drunks can be dangerous?" He was so mad, his eyes were shooting darts at her. She looked at him and saw he was livid. She had tried so hard to do well, but his anger was her undoing. She stared but didn't say a word in her own defense, as he continued to rant at her. "It's a wonder you didn't get yourself hurt. When are you going to stop trying to solve problems by yourself? Chuck said he tried to get you to wait and let him go with you."

She could stand it no longer. She laid her head on her arms and sobbed.

James softened. "Ah, Meg, what in the world am I doing to you? I know you did your best, but I was so afraid for you when I thought what could have happened. I'm sorry I yelled at you." He walked to the desk and pulled her into his arms as if he would never let her go. She clung to him and snuggled into his embrace. He ran his hand over her hair and rubbed her back, trying to comfort her. His anguish for her was evident in his touch. "It's okay. Go ahead and cry it out. Get it out of your system. I can't imagine the terror you felt when that drunk landed on you. If he would have done anything to you, I would have … I would have … I don't know what I would have done, but it wouldn't have been very Christian." His agony for her sounded worse than her hurt. She raised her head and looked into eyes, which pierced hers with understanding and compassion. "I'm so sorry, Meg. The last thing you needed after your ordeal last night was for me to yell at you. Will you forgive me?"

She could only nod before she returned to the comfort of his embrace. He rocked her gently back and forth as he held her to him. Finally, she pulled away. When she did, he lifted her chin and tenderly kissed her. Her bruised lips felt no pain but tingled with pleasure.

"Meg, what am I going to do about you?" He felt her stiffen. The comfort she had drawn from him seemed to dissipate.

"I'm sorry, too. I was a little overcome by those guys last night. Let me tell you what else has been going on."

The shell she'd placed around her heart had slid back into place as she told him about the uneventful happenings of the other days.

Chapter Six

*M*EG SAW LITTLE of James for the remainder of the day, but the morning's episode had had a big impact on her. At supper that evening, she hoped he would sit by her, but he was a no-show.

Mattie, however, did come to her table. "May I join you, Meg? I've had a busy day with kids and could use some adult conversation."

"Did that group of Girl Scouts bombard the snack shack today?"

Mattie nodded. "I don't care if I ever see another ice cream or snow cone again. I didn't know a bunch of girls could eat so much. They giggled, yelled, and dropped stuff on the floor. Their troop leaders sat on the benches by the tree while I was working my fingers into icicles."

"Poor Mattie." Despite her words, Meg did not sound at all sympathetic to her friend's plight. She kept glancing at the door, hoping to see James. "I'm so relieved James is back, but I'd still like to see him to confirm that he's not the mirage I imagined."

"No reason to explain further. I understand completely."

Meg could feel the flush moving up her face.

"Just as I hoped," Mattie went on. "You missed the guy. There might be hope for you two yet."

About that time, James walked in the door, got his food tray, and headed directly for their table. He returned Meg's smile. "Mattie … Meg. How did you two do today?"

Mattie recounted the story of the Girl Scouts, still overwhelmed by their behavior.

Since it was a table for only two, James sat conspicuously in the space between tables rolling his spaghetti onto his fork.

"I don't know how you do that," Meg commented. "I give up and cut mine."

He demonstrated again as Meg shook her head in bewilderment. "It just won't work for me."

"Never give up." He shot Meg a look only she understood. James was talking about more than spaghetti as he winked at her. "It actually took me several meals to learn how to roll the spaghetti. My mom would say to me, 'James, if you're going to amount to anything in this life, you've got to remember that God is always there to help you. When you know something is right, don't quit trying 'til you've accomplished what He wants.'"

Mattie, totally unaware of his hidden meaning, said increduously, "I can't believe your mother taught you that God was with you when you were trying to learn how to eat spaghetti."

"He's with us in everything we do, Mattie," James said. "Nothing's too big for Him, and nothing's too small for Him to care." After a while Mattie excused herself, and James moved to her chair to get out of the aisle. "When I finish eating, would you go for a walk with me?" he asked Meg.

James and Meg were walking toward the path the hay wagon travelled when he asked, "Is it okay with you if we walk the whole trail? I want to talk to somebody about my sister, and it may take a while to get it out." He reached for her hand. Smiling at her tenderly, he patted it with his free hand but didn't speak.

For several minutes, they walked in companionable silence. He reached down, plucked some Queen Anne's lace, and handed it to her. "This reminds me of you—intricate, complicated, and beautiful."

Meg smiled, "I'm not as complicated as you think but thank you."

As they topped a little ridge, a break in the tree line brought the sunset into view. "Isn't it spectacular tonight?" James said. The horizon was filled with streaks of gold and orange. The light, feathery clouds lingering over the sunset would have been a painter's delight. Still holding her hand, he sat on a log, and she sat beside him. "Let's watch the sunset a while. It won't last long, and after the last few days, I need something peaceful to absorb. Seeing it makes me realize God is still in control and all is well, even if I don't understand why He took Amy."

"Why didn't you tell me about Amy?" Meg asked quietly.

He turned slightly away from Meg, rested his elbows on his knees, and propped his chin on his hands. He seemed totally lost in his thoughts and completely unaware of her presence.

"Do you want to talk about her?" Meg asked.

He said nothing, but Meg saw his shoulders begin to shake. She put her hand on his back and thought she understood his heartache but felt powerless to help him. He did not make a sound, but she knew James was weeping for his little sister. For long minutes, they sat there, her hand rubbing his back, as the strong man beside her wept. At last he spoke. "I'm sorry. I didn't come out here to act like a baby."

"Look at me." When he ignored her, Meg took his chin and turned his face toward hers in a manner that was so compassionate, he longed to be comforted by her. "Jesus wept when his friend Lazarus died. Don't you think if Jesus could weep over a friend, it's okay for you to weep over your sister?"

"It's not just Amy. It hasn't been that long since Mom died, and it has all caught up with me. We've known since Amy was tiny that this could happen any time, but we had tried not to think about it. One person at the funeral said, 'God just needed another angel.' Another said He wanted a flower in his heavenly bouquet, like she wasn't even human. I wanted to punch both of them. Amy was a person who was severely handicapped, but she was made special. God loved her, and so did we. I didn't want her to die. She was always so glad to see me. She'd wobble to me and say, 'Dames … Dames … lift me high.'" James sighed and took a deep breath before continuing. "I'd lift her to the ceiling, and she'd giggle that special little laugh of hers. When I was down in the dumps, her consistently sweet attitude would make me ashamed of myself."

James continued to tell about Amy. "She taught me as much about God's love as my church did. She was always dependable and faithful to love me, just like God is with us. One night, I sat discussing some theological point with my dad. I had gotten confused about this subject, but Amy looked at me with her innocent eyes. 'God loves you, Dames. God loves Amy too,' she said. I never did figure out the theological problem, but I did go to bed thinking about what Amy said. I knew God loved me enough to die for me, even if I had been the only person who ever lived. I don't have to understand everything. I only have to believe He loves me. Does what I'm saying make sense?"

"It does. I think Amy knew all that was necessary to know about God. He lets the simple understand and confounds the wise. Some people overthink the gospel."

The sunset was giving way to darkness. The night air was cool, and Meg shivered.

"We'd better get back to the cabins since we didn't bring jackets. Thanks for letting me talk," he said.

When she stood beside him, he started to put his arms around her. She automatically went into his embrace. At first, his kiss was gentle, but with Meg's obvious response to it, he kissed her hungrily. Meg's senses soared beyond her imagination.

At last, he stepped away. "We've got to go back," he repeated but not before he slipped in one more quick kiss. She looked deeply into his eyes and saw that the feelings he had for her had a depth that both delighted and frightened her.

"I'll race you," she said brightly to lighten the atmosphere. She took off running the trail back to the campground.

James, more relaxed since talking about his sister, took out after her. After a short run, Meg began to get winded and slowed down. "Let's stop. I'm running out of breath."

"I never know what to expect from you," James said, stopping beside her. "You took off like a dog chasing a rabbit, and now you're tired already. Are you out of shape?"

"I am. I haven't run like that for months. Can we please walk?"

He put his arm over her shoulders so that she had to move closer to him. With her arm around his waist, they chatted freely for the remainder of the way to the campground.

When they got to Meg's cabin, he told her he had things to do. She had hoped for another embrace and kiss but was disappointed when they didn't come.

"Thanks for letting me talk about Amy," James said. "I needed that." He squeezed her hand and walked into the night.

As she leisurely prepared for bed and then settled between the sheets, she thought of James. He was certainly consuming a lot of her thoughts these days.

———

When Meg's day off came, she got an inner tube from the storage area and joined the first bus load going for a tube float. They would travel upriver from the resort about three miles. She was looking forward to a lazy day of relaxation on the river.

As she was about to take her seat, she heard her name called and recognized one of the staff.

"Come sit with me," he called to her.

"Is this your day off too, Dave?"

"Sure thing, and I was ready after the last few days. It's been hectic around here."

"I'm ready to relax on the river. Those three days of being in charge got to me," Meg responded.

"I heard about the episode with the drunks. Chuck was waiting to tell James about it the second he arrived back from the funeral. I couldn't hear what was said, but James was sure upset. He took off for his office at a run and left Chuck standing."

"I really don't want to talk about it. I'd just like to forget the whole incident. I will tell you, though, that those guys scared me half to death."

"Sorry. I didn't want to bring up a tough subject. I won't mention it again. I'm by myself today. Do you want to float with me?" Dave asked.

"Sure. If I get caught in some driftwood, you can get me loose. But you've got to promise to not talk about anything that makes me think. I'm here strictly for relaxation."

"It's a deal. We won't solve a single world problem."

In order to stay close together, Dave used the rope, which he had brought to hold his sodas to the inner tube. After connecting the two tubes with the rope, Dave carried both tubes as they walked into the water. "Oh, the water's cold this morning."

The river moved swiftly as they tried to sit in their tubes. Each time they attempted to board their tubes, the current would move the tubes away from them. Dave finally jumped into his tube and motioned for Meg to do the same. She barely got seated before the current sped them downstream.

"I love this river," Meg said. "It smells so fresh. Maybe I appreciate it so much because I've been teaching in the city with smog and gas fumes."

They floated out of the current to a slower section of the river. Only when the water was too shallow to float over the rapids did they get out of their tubes. Their sneaker-clad feet easily maneuvered the rocks until they could seat themselves again. By noon, they had traveled half of the five-mile float and had reached the resort's gravel bar.

"I brought a granola bar for lunch," Meg said. "Every summer I gain weight on Ginger's cooking and can't get back into my school clothes in the fall. I'm trying to keep from doing that this year."

When Dave handed her an apple, though, she gladly took it and munched it hungrily.

Dave told Meg that her back was getting red—always a problem with the sun reflecting off the water. After applying as much sunscreen to her back as she could reach, she asked him to finish it.

At the loud backfire of a truck, which Meg thought was a gun, she jumped up and fell into Dave's lap. He was trying to help her get off him but both were laughing too hard to accomplish it.

"Dave … Meg," James said as he came up behind them. "It looks like you two are certainly having a good time." He looked directly at Meg, daring her to deny the fact.

"Yes, we are, thank you." Her response was as brittle as the look he'd given her. It was obvious to Meg that James thought she and Dave had planned this outing to be together today. She decided to let him think it. After their evening stroll, she was having second thoughts about their relationship. She did not want James to know how much she cared for him. The anger—or maybe it was hurt—she saw in his face made her turn her face toward the river. She hoped the guilt for pretending to be with Dave would go away as quickly as the driftwood she saw floating down the river.

"Dave, could you eat breakfast with me tomorrow morning?" James asked.

After Dave agreed, James nodded to Meg and went toward the river bank to pick up some canoes brought in by campers who did not want to continue to travel the ten-mile canoe float.

Meg did not see James staring as she and Dave floated off after lunch, but Dave did. "I wonder what's wrong with James," Dave said. "He seemed out of sorts about something. You'd think I'd just stolen his girlfriend."

Meg could not help the redness that came to her face. She hated to blush but was unable to control the flush that always came when she was embarrassed.

"Oh, great!" Dave immediately knew why James wanted to have breakfast with him the next morning. "Guess I'm in trouble with the boss for floating with you today. Should I tell him I'm engaged, and we just met on the bus and decided to float together?"

"Don't worry about it. He knows I have no intentions of getting serious with anyone. I've told him that, and if he thinks I'm his girlfriend, then that's his problem."

Dave wondered if Meg was trying to convince herself more than him. "If you say not to worry about it, I won't. I know it's your business, but it seems to me like you could do a lot worse than James. He's actually a good guy. The other day he was telling me about his plans to work in the inner city after he graduates from seminary. He said he might have to pastor somewhere else first, to get some experience under his belt, before he tackles the challenges of the inner city. I bet he's going to be quite a fireball when he's working with those inner-city kids. He'll be one tough cookie for them to encounter."

"I've never heard a pastor described with those terms, but I have a feeling you're right. He will be loving but strict with the kids. You know Bert would have been in sad shape this summer if James hadn't agreed to take charge here."

"Did you hear they moved Bert this morning to an acute care center here in our area?" he asked changing the subject.

"Great. I'm so glad he'll be closer. It just doesn't seem right for him not to be around. He always gives my ego a boost. Hearing him talk, you'd think that he couldn't run the place without me."

"You too? I've heard several yearly workers say the same thing. The man's got a real knack of working with people. He makes us all think we're indispensable and that makes us willing to work all that much harder for him."

After the float, Meg headed for the showers and then to her cabin to rest. When she awakened, it was dark, and supper was already over. Realizing this, she turned over and went back to sleep.

When she opened her eyes the next morning, raindrops were falling on the roof. As she peered out her window, she saw James walking toward the dining hall for breakfast.

If I hurry, I can eat with him. She slipped into jeans and a green shirt, which made her eyes shine. She ran the brush through her hair, pulled it back, and tied a green ribbon around her ponytail to match her shirt. After stealing a quick glance in the mirror, she was out the door and soon wished she'd grabbed her umbrella.

Disappointment hit her when she saw James and Dave having what appeared to be a serious conversation. *Oh, great, I forgot they were eating breakfast together,* Meg thought. Then she saw her friend. "Good morning, Mattie. Do you want to eat with me?"

Meg ate a large breakfast, and Mattie told her she would get bigger than the side of a barn if she kept eating at that pace.

"I missed supper last night, so I was famished, but I think I've caught up what I missed."

"I hope so," said a familiar deep voice behind her. "If not, you'll eat all the profits Bert's going to make this summer." James had seen her plate loaded with food and was now enjoying teasing her.

Meg was glad to see James wasn't mad about the previous day's float with Dave. She smiled and asked how Bert was doing after his transfer to the acute care center close to the resort. "I'd love to see him, again."

"How about tonight? I planned to go over after supper, and you're welcome to come with me," James said.

Meg, dressed in a navy-blue skirt, white peasant blouse, and sandals, was ready when James called for her.

"Hm-m-m, you look good," he said as he opened the car door for her. "I don't know if I've ever seen you in a skirt. I like the feminine touch."

Pleased with the compliment, she had a feeling the evening was going to be a good one, and it lived up to her expectations. Bert was his usual teasing self during the visit and made a few comments about seeing the two of them together again. Meg, more comfortable with James than she had been on their first visit to see Bert, enjoyed his attempts at cultivating their romance.

When they returned to the resort, Meg expected James to kiss her good night, but again, he didn't. In fact, he hadn't even held her hand during the entire evening. She was slightly irked to think that he had not touched her throughout their time together.

Meg could not explain her depression. She knew she would never allow herself to fall in love, but now that James wasn't attempting to reach out to her, she was dismayed. *Men … I will never understand them.* Those she had not liked had been all hands around her, but now that she wanted to be touched, James was not doing so. *How does the male brain work anyway? And what in the world is wrong with me? James is doing exactly what I asked him to do, but it doesn't make me happy.*

At the general store the next day, James crept quietly behind her and tapped her shoulder, which made her jump.

"James Carson, don't you ever do that again! You just about scared six inches off my height."

He looked her over. "I like what I see, so it's a good thing I didn't do that."

"Is that right?" she asked, aware that she had a flirtatious lilt to her voice.

"It is, and, furthermore, you're glad I like your looks, aren't you?"

"If you say so."

"You'd rather die than admit you like me, even a little," James challenged.

"That isn't true," she insisted.

"Then say it."

"It."

"You know exactly what I want you to say. Now repeat after me, 'I like you.'" When she didn't respond, he said, "I'm waiting, Meg."

She was cornered. "What's bugging you this morning and why do you want me to say I like you. Sure, I like you … similar to the way I like Bill."

"Monica Elizabeth Green, my patience is wearing thin."

So she said, with total lack of feeling in her voice, "I like you."

"Not exactly the tone of voice I would have liked, but I guess I'll have to settle for what I can get. Now that you've said what I wanted you to say, how about sitting in the projection room with me tonight while we show the weekly movie?"

"Are you sure you want me?"

"I've never been more certain of anything in my life. I'll see you at 8:30."

Meg thought about the ridiculous conversation they'd just finished. She knew she liked James more than any of the other men she had dated. If things were different, she could get serious about him, but things weren't different, and they never would be. She was stuck with her fate. Resigned to the fact, she drew a deep breath and stared out the window but saw nothing.

Back in his office, James watched Meg. He surmised she was thinking about their relationship. He knew he'd been a bit demanding a few minutes earlier, but he hoped by having her say the words, she would think about them and realize she actually did care for him. Someday, he hoped she would love him, and he prayed to that end.

Meg stepped into the projection room above the general store just as it was starting to get dark outside. James didn't lift his head when she came in but continued to concentrate on the old projector. Seeing he was absorbed in his task, she asked, "What's wrong?"

"I don't know. I hate this thing. It's antiquated and isn't working right. I don't know why Bert can't enter the modern era of electronics?"

"Let me do it. I had to learn to run a projector at school." She scooted James out of her way and began rewinding the reel. When Meg finished, she grinned at him triumphantly. "It will run right now. The film wasn't tight enough around the reel." The quick peck she got on her cheek made her previous effort worth each minute she worked.

"Thanks, I would have been here a long time trying to figure out how to rewind that thing. This projector is ancient," he again complained. "It would be nice if Bert would replace these old films with DVDs or Blu-Ray."

Meg looked from the second story window and saw that the group gathering to watch the movie was growing. The lawn in front of the general store was filled with lawn chairs and blankets as people spread out on the grass. The "screen" had last year's patches on the four king-size sheets that were sewn together.

"What's the movie tonight?" Meg asked.

"I picked a Disney classic. Do you remember the one about the talking car?"

"Herbie is the car's name. I love that movie. It'll be fun to watch it again and see the kids enjoy it."

He walked to the window to see the crowd. "It looks like we've got about a hundred folks out tonight. Mrs. Waterman has brought her poodles."

"What if her mutts start barking during the movie?"

"Shame, shame. Mrs. Waterman wouldn't appreciate your calling her hybrid dogs 'mutts.'"

"Most of the time I like poodles, but those two are spoiled rotten. She takes them everywhere. One of them almost turned the canoe over when he saw a squirrel."

"I would have liked to have seen that. How was she dressed for the float?"

"She had yellow polka-dot shorts, a bright red shirt, and a straw hat with a ribbon around the brim to match her blouse, and yellow spiked sandals." Meg thought Mrs. Waterman was one of the most unusual guests they'd ever had visit. She felt for the woman's husband because he had to put up with her and the dogs. He seemed to adore her, though, so it must have not bothered him nearly as much as it did Meg.

"It's about dark out there. Let's get this show on the road. Lights ... camera ... action. Pull your chair beside me, and you'll be able to see the movie."

Meg counted the patches on the sheet screen. "The sheets have seven patches this year. Once the movie starts, the patches get lost in the story," Meg said.

James didn't know if she was talking to him or the guests sitting on the lawn, though they weren't close enough to hear her. "Sh-h-h, I want to watch the movie too."

Meg gradually leaned toward James for a better view of the screen. He put his arm around her and drew her close to his side. "Now can you see better?"

"Yes, thank you." Meg didn't tell him she was now distracted from the movie. Instead, she cuddled closer to him, but James, who was totally absorbed in the story, seemed oblivious to her presence. He was thoroughly enjoying Herbie's antics and laughing at each one of them.

Soon Meg also got interested in the story and relaxed beside James. During a slow scene, he whispered, "You're right where you belong—beside me. Are you enjoying it?"

"The movie or being next to you?"

"Both." Although it was almost dark in the projection room, James had enough light from the projector to see her eyes begin to twinkle with mischief. He knew some sort of wisecrack was forthcoming. "There's only one way to stop a wisecrack," he said before she could speak. With his left hand, he brushed back her hair and then thoroughly kissed her. "Mm-m-m, good lipstick."

Meg pulled away from him. "That's all you can say?"

"I've got a whole lot more I'd like to say to you, but the time's not right. You're not ready to hear what I want to say."

"What do you mean by that?"

"We're getting along fairly well right now, but I know there's something about our relationship that still bothers you. You're on your guard around me, and until you can trust me enough to talk about whatever is going through that pretty head of yours, I think it's best for me to keep my thoughts to myself." The first part of the movie ended just as James stopped talking. "I need to change the reel," Meg said as the old projector came to a stop. Now she didn't have to respond to his comment.

"While you do that, I'll go get us some popcorn and soda."

When the second half began, Meg intended to stay in her seat and not lean toward James, but laughter from the crowd below again brought her to lean against him so she could see what was funny on the screen.

"I was wondering how long you were going to stay over there," he said as he drew her back to him.

When she started to say something, James put his fingers over her lips to quiet her. She decided she could sit beside him and enjoy the movie, or she could be disagreeable. The former won her internal argument. When his arm went to the back of her chair, she again snuggled close to him. She was absorbed in the movie and missed the occasional glances he sent her way.

He could not figure her out. *I know she likes me, but I just don't understand her hesitancy to become more involved. Did a relationship go sour with a man she cared about? That couldn't be, because Bill would have known about that. Maybe she's afraid she'll get hurt. That doesn't seem reasonable either, for someone as strong-willed as Meg.* Eventually, he stopped trying to figure it out and decided the only thing to do was talk to God about it. *Lord,* he prayed silently. *I don't know what her fear is, but would You teach her that perfect love casts out fear. I've done all I know to do to let her know how much I care for her. Help her, please. And while You're at it, give me the patience I need.*

Meg laughed at one of Herbie's stunts. "Aren't you watching the movie?" she asked when he didn't laugh too.

"I was praying."

"You sure chose a strange place for prayer. Sorry if I interrupted." She quickly diverted her attention back to the movie, cuddled closer, and didn't question him further.

The next day neither James nor Meg mentioned the previous evening. She was certain he'd pay more attention to her, but instead, she barely saw him. Usually, he would at least stop to chat for a minute, but today he was busy running from one task to the next.

The mid-summer temperatures began to soar, and so did tempers during the next few days. Guests were grumpy and a few were just plain hateful. It took all of Meg's inner strength to be polite to a few of them. She sold more sunscreen in three days than she had during all the month of June. Groups coming in were interested mostly in the water activities and then came back from the floats, complaining about their sunburn.

"The river's getting low," one customer complained. "We spent as much time carrying our canoe as floating the water. It's not much fun that way."

"That's common in the heat of the summer, when we haven't had much rain," she offered to the disgruntled guest.

"Next time I want to come, I'm going to check the water level before I make a reservation."

Firewood, which was always available free of charge, stayed stacked. Only those cooking over an open fire came to get it.

James came in the store after being out for a couple of hours. His shirt was soaked, and sweat ran down his face, which was reddened by the intense heat. "Be sure to warn everyone who comes in here to keep a close eye on their fires. It's so dry out there that the whole place could go up in flames if someone gets careless."

Although she was disappointed he didn't stay to talk, Meg began to make fire warning posters to hang around the campground. She turned the radio on and heard the news giving the same warning. The weekend forecast, however, called for rain. She hoped there wouldn't be any incidents before then.

She got a snow cone from Mattie's snack shack as she hung the fire warning posters. On her way to put up one poster, she saw two children playing with matches. After thoroughly scolding them, she continued walking. Their parents had heard her and called the children to them, where they again were scolded, and the matches were taken away from them.

During one of his quick trips to the store, James asked Meg who had put up the fire warning posters.

"Your hard-working PR director, sir," Meg said, making an extremely deep bow.

"Well done, little one." He patted her shoulder as he hurried out the door again.

Now Meg was happy. She was always pleased when James called her "little one," since her stature was far from tiny. He knew how to boost her ego--that was for sure.

As forecast, steady rains came on the weekend, making a general mess of the campground but bringing a sigh of relief from the staff, who had been on constant alert for out-of-control fires.

Meg was getting ready to close the store for the evening when James walked through the door and plopped in the old rocking chair. "I'm wiped out! Am I ever glad there aren't a lot of weeks like this one has been. The weatherman is saying we've got some cooler days ahead, and I hope he hits the nail on the head this time. This sweltering heat gets to me. Let's celebrate the rain and promise of cooler weather by going to town and grabbing a burger and fries."

"Sounds good to me. I'm ready to get away for a while too. The customers have been cranky. Give me a few minutes to freshen up."

"Twenty minutes is all you get. I'm hungry as a bear."

Meg looked at herself in the mirror. She knotted the tail of her red-and-white checked blouse and let it hang over her jeans shorts. Since it was still stifling hot with the high humidity, she pulled her hair back into what seemed to be her ever-present ponytail. Seeing the red ribbon in her drawer, she tied it around her hair. "I look like I'm about sixteen years old … oh, well, who cares?"

When James knocked on her door a few minutes later, his hair was still wet from the shower, but he looked fresh and cool in his shorts and T-shirt. "Say," he said as he gently tugged her ponytail, "you look cute."

"Cute? That's a word my high school students use."

"With that outfit, you look like you're in high school. I like it. It shows off your sassy personality."

"With that remark you're going to be in trouble before we get out the door." She acted like she was going to give him a little punch on his arm, but when she attempted to do it, he grabbed her hand, brought it to his lips, and kissed it.

"Let's go. I'm starving," he said.

"Can I have a shake too?"

"As cute as you look, you could probably get me to give you a new car if you asked for it."

His praise made her glow and brought out the good mood she was feeling. She loved to spend time with James, who in so many ways seemed to be her perfect match.

At the hamburger joint, they sat eating their meal and talked with an easy camaraderie. When Meg gave him her dill pickle, he nibbled at her fingers, forcing her to stifle a giggle.

On the way back to the resort, Meg stared out the car window.

She realized that she and James had much common ground, which made it easy for them to talk.

Before they reached the resort, James pulled into a dark spot along the road and pulled her to him. He reached for the ribbon around her hair and casually took it off. When she tried to take the ribbon, he said, "Leave it alone. I like your hair down. Beautiful hair should be down to be seen." He moved his hands away from hers and ran his fingers through her long blonde tresses.

Meg shivered at his touch and looked directly at him. For long seconds, their eyes met, and each read the unmistakable message of the other. James bent his head to her waiting lips. He drew her closer and again ran his fingers through her hair. "If you only knew what you do to me, little one." Again, his lips found hers and then made their way to her neck. Suddenly, he stiffened. "Let's go. We surely can't stay here and keep doing this."

She reached for his hand, squeezed it, and grinned at him.

Truth hit Meg like a hammer blow. She had not kept her guard up around this man and now had to admit she loved him. To make matters even worse, she was almost certain he felt the same way about her. Both of their hearts were going to be broken, because her situation had not changed. Still, she knew there were not many weeks left of her summer break, and she simply could not stop spending time with him. She didn't have the self-control to turn him away when she needed and loved him so much. But she knew beyond any doubt that she was only setting up both of them for more hurt when the season ended and they went back to their schools.

"Are you having happy thoughts?" James asked.

"Maybe."

"Want to tell me what you're thinking about?"

Meg shook her head. "No way—a good woman doesn't kiss and tell." Since she had decided she would continue to date James for the remainder of the summer, she began chatting about nothing in particular and everything in general.

He was enjoying this lighter side of Meg. "I don't know what's changed, but you're acting differently. I like this side of you."

Meg would not tell him of her decision to continue to date him. For just this once, she decided, she would date a man and become a bit more involved with him. She only hoped he wouldn't be too hurt when she told him at the end of the summer that their relationship had to end. That was another day, though, and she just wouldn't think about it now.

<center>~~~~~~~~~</center>

The next afternoon, James said he was going to take a couple of days off work and go camping at Wapapello Lake. "When I saw Bert yesterday, he insisted I should have some time off. I asked him if you could go with me to Wapapello. The old codger burst out laughing, gave my leg a hard pat, and assured me it would be fine. I think he's trying to be a matchmaker."

Meg was truly glad James was going to have some time off, but she was slightly puzzled about why he would want her to go during his break. "What are you planning on doing while you're there?"

"I want to spend more time with you. I enjoy your company, and as far as what I'm going to be doing … practically nothing, except maybe a little fishing and swimming. I'm going to enjoy this break and am hoping you'll share it with me."

"You're planning on camping?" Meg questioned.

"Of course. What did you think I planned to do?"

Meg didn't want to admit where her thoughts had gone, so she just blurted out, "What about … where would we sleep?"

"Monica Elizabeth Green! I ought to ring your neck for even asking such a thing. You've worked with me for two months. I've kissed you many times but wanted to kiss you a lot more. I've controlled myself around you, yet you wonder about my intentions." He stared at her a moment and then continued. "I thought you would know by now I'd not do anything immoral with you or any other woman. I've already got two small tents borrowed. We will not be sleeping together, but we will be together during our waking hours."

Meg felt a bit ashamed of herself. She didn't want James to see the tears in her eyes. She should have known she could trust him when she'd seen him hold back, knowing he wanted more from her. When a tear dropped from her cheek, he apologized to her.

"I'm sorry I asked you to come along. Just forget the whole thing. I'll go by myself."

"I'm glad you asked me to go with you." She smiled at him through her tears.

"Then why are you crying?"

"Because I know I don't need to worry when I'm with you. You're strong enough for both of us."

"It's not my strength, Meg. It's God's strength. When I am weak, He is strong. I'm just as frail as any other man and have the same desires. Do you understand what I'm trying to say to you?"

"I think I do, and I'm learning how much you depend on the Lord in your daily life. If the offer is still open, I'd like to go with you."

Chapter Seven

*M*EG NOTICED THE car clock registered 10:00 when they pulled into Redman Campground two mornings later. Fortunately, Meg did not have any difficulty finding someone to work the general store while she was gone. Planning for the trip had been fun, as she and James made lists of everything they thought they would need, borrowed cooking utensils from the resort kitchen, packed the car, and finally got off to Wapapello early Friday morning. They would not have to be back until Monday morning, since they had managed to get replacements for three days.

Looking for a level campsite to place their tents, Meg noticed there was no litter lying around any of the sites. The RV spots were mostly full and only a few tent places remained.

"It looks like we'll have to camp by those walk-in spots," James said. "Sorry we couldn't get closer, but I like a level place for the tents. There's going to be a lot of stuff to carry."

"It's not that far from the parking area to the campsite. With both of us working, we should have everything there in just a few minutes."

Just as Meg had predicted, the car was unloaded and the campsite filled with their stuff with just a few trips. They were able to get just one campsite, thanks to a kind manager who didn't make them rent two spots for two tents, as was customary at some campgrounds. When the manager noticed the absence of wedding rings, he was pleased to see they had two tents, so showed his appreciation of their moral standing.

"Let's get these tents set up and our sleeping mats and bags in place. By then we'll be ready for some lunch." Both of them began taking things from their bags when James said, "Whoa. If we empty both tent bags, we won't know which poles go with each tent. We'll do yours first and then mine. Let me give you a hand." With that, he pushed the things he'd pulled out back into his bag. James laid the poles down and reached for the blue-and-green canvas. "Have you ever done this before?"

"I've watched Dad and Bill. We used to camp a lot."

"You make that sound like its past tense. Doesn't your family camp anymore?"

"No ... not anymore since Mom's ... no, we don't camp now."

James wanted to question her more but decided against it. What did she not want to tell him? James slid the flexible rods through the slots in the canvas and set the small domed tent down. "All set except for the pegs. That was easy. Now let's get mine up." James' tent was not like the lightweight one he had borrowed for Meg. As he began to pull the poles and rods from his bag, he noticed the odor coming from the bag. "These old canvas things smell like mildew," he said. Even with Meg's help, it took over thirty minutes to set up the older, smelly tent, but it was considerably larger than Meg's.

"You've got a bigger tent than I do, and I've got the most stuff. No fair," Meg teased.

"I'll trade you size for smell."

"No thanks ... I know when I've got a good thing going."

When both tents were up, he put four tent pegs in the outside corners of each to hold them down in case a strong wind should blow.

They added the pads and sleeping bags to the tents and

then their small pieces of luggage. For three days, this would be home.

They got a picnic tablecloth out of a plastic bin, put it over the table, and added the water jug and food items secured in their animal-proof containers. They were ready for their lunch.

James started a small campfire that would be just big enough to roast the hot dogs Ginger had sent with them. "Food is so good when it's cooked over an open fire. I want another one." As he spoke, James took another hot dog for each of them and then roasted them to perfection.

While drinking their sodas, they munched on the cookies Ginger had also sent. After thoroughly stuffing themselves, James suggested they get into their swimsuits and walk to the swimming beach at the lake. It would be a thirty-minute walk but by then they'd be ready to swim.

"Come on, pokey," Meg said, hitting the side of the other tent. "I'm ready to go."

"We'll see who can get back up the hill fastest after we swim," James returned.

With towels around their shoulders, they headed down the hill. When they reached the lake, Meg spread her towel on the sand and lay down. "Go ahead and swim. I'm going to take a nap." She turned onto her stomach and closed her eyes.

She heard James splash into the water but quickly fell fast asleep. When she felt water dripping on her, she slid the towel away from her eyes and saw bare feet. Looking upward, she saw James was grinning at her.

"Are you going to sleep all day or go swimming with me?" As she stood up, James said, "You'd better turn around so I can get some sunscreen on your back. You're getting red."

"How long have I been asleep?"

"Long enough. Those girls are annoying me." He pointed to three teenage girls. "I need you to come into the water to protect me from them."

Meg thought he was teasing, but when she saw the three shapely teens in bikinis sneaking up behind him, she realized he was serious. "You're about to get caught," she whispered.

"Come on, Meg, help me out. Those three have been pestering me for ten minutes. I can't get rid of them."

Meg, now wide awake, tackled James and fell beside him. The girls were watching as he awkwardly landed. She reached over him and thoroughly kissed him.

He said through clenched teeth. "You're going to pay for tackling me, but I sure liked the results."

"Hey, I was just helping you out, and it worked. The girls are leaving to find someone else to bother."

James straightened and stretched beside her. After a few minutes he said, "I'm going swimming again."

"Then I'll go with you. I'm not much of a sun worshipper, and I'm hot lying here. I'd rather get my tan while I'm swimming or working."

They swam for almost an hour before James pronounced her back too red and said if they didn't get out of the water, she was going to be miserable.

Back at the campsite, Meg changed into her shorts and blouse and pulled her hair again into a pony tail. She applied only a bit of lipstick, knowing her sun-reddened cheeks were making her skin glow.

Relaxing in the lounge chairs gave them time to chat with one another as the birds entertained them with their chirping. Deciding it was time to eat again, Meg began opening a can of pork and beans.

"I'll get the fire going so I can grill some burgers," James said as he began setting the firewood into position. "The fire will be ready in about fifteen minutes. Are we having plain pork and beans, or are you going to add barbeque sauce to them?"

They both decided they wanted barbequed beans instead of plain ones, so Meg got them ready to add to the pot they had brought to sit over the fire. She had peeled and sliced potatoes and onions which were sizzling in the iron skillet. When she was slicing the fresh garden tomatoes they'd purchased at a roadside vegetable stand, she complained, "We haven't even started to eat, and the flies and ants are already coming. Sure wish I knew why God made those pests."

James quoted, "'Take a lesson from the ants, you lazybones. Learn from her ways and be wise!' That's Proverbs 6:6" (NLT)

"I'd forgotten about that verse," Meg admitted. "The next time I see an ant hill, I'll study them, but for now I'm going to get the outdoor insect repellent and spray around the table."

After their supper, James asked if she wanted to go fishing with him or stay at the campsite and read a book she'd brought along.

"I'll go if you bait my hook."

"Don't tell me you're one of those squeamish females. I didn't expect that from you."

Looking slightly ashamed, she admitted, "I just can't stand pushing the hook through the worm's guts. It's gross."

"You're not as tough or hard-hearted as I thought you were." He put his arm over her shoulders and led her to the boat dock.

"Do you really think I'm hard-hearted?" she asked.

"Nope. We'll have to rent everything since I didn't have any of my fishing gear at the resort. I thought since I was taking Bert's place, I wouldn't have a moment to set a hook in the water."

The bait shop had the equipment they needed. James not only purchased worms but added a few crickets to his bait. "I think we'll go back up close to the campsite, where that cove is. I noticed earlier it looked like a good spot to catch some bass. There were some trees down in the water. That's just the kind of spots where bass like to hide."

"I like crappie better than bass. Bass are too boney. Dad and Bill wouldn't fish for much besides crappie. They'd filet them, and I loved them." Meg chattered while James got the stuff in the boat.

James pulled on the cord to start the boat's motor and almost lost his balance as the cord broke. Meg saw the aggravation on his face as he took the broken cord to the bait shop.

In a few minutes, he was back. "We're changing boats. Would you believe the guy gave me five dollars back because the cord broke? That was pretty decent of him. I guess he didn't want to lose our business."

They gathered their fishing gear and went to the assigned boat. Once they were on the lake, they sat quietly, throwing their lines into the water. Meg was the first to feel a tug on her line. James saw the line pull and said, "You've got one. Bring him in nice and easy."

Slowly, Meg began reeling it in until the fish cleared the water. "Look at that! He's big enough for our supper tomorrow night. I can't believe I actually caught a fish."

James grabbed the net and scooped the fish into it. "He must be a pound at least. I guess you know I am thoroughly jealous of your getting the first fish."

Meg beamed at his praise. "I've caught a few little guys but nothing like this fine fella. I think I'd rather mount him than eat him."

"Forget that. I want fried fish tomorrow."

The remainder of the evening passed quickly, and Meg was silently relieved when James also caught a nice bass—even if it wasn't quite a big as hers. When they added another one to their catch, James called it an evening, saying there wasn't any use to catch them if they couldn't eat them.

James started another fire so they could roast marshmallows and have s'mores. Meg liked her marshmallows burned and ate only those blackened by the flames. James ate one barely brown marshmallow and then made himself two s'mores. He began telling stories that his fellow seminary students had told about mishaps at weddings. Meg was laughing so hard, she was holding her sides. "I sure hope nothing like that happens at my wedding … if I were going to have a wedding," she added quickly.

"You can have one."

"No, I can't."

"Why, Meg? Are you so against men that you can't stand the thought of living with one of us?"

"It's not that at all. There are just some things I can't explain."

"If you'll try, I promise not to interrupt or comment until you're finished talking."

She shook her head but looked at him with such hurt in her eyes, it was all he could do to keep from getting up and taking her in his arms. He didn't know how to get her to talk about the problem, so he said nothing. He could only wait.

Meg looked at the ground as her face saddened, but she didn't say a word.

He watched her for a long time and finally said so very tenderly, "Meg …"

She looked at him then but shook her head. "It's no use, James. Things are the way they are, and nothing can change the facts. It's just not fair …"

"If you would tell me what the situation is, perhaps together we could work at a solution."

"I read all about it. Nothing can be done. It's useless to try."

"Do you mean the problem has nothing to do with you personally?"

"Of course it has something to do with me," she said with total dismay. "Not personally to do with me, but it affects me." She thought the sigh she heard from James sounded like relief. She wished so much that she could tell him the problem. Instead, she stood, saying, "I think I'd better go to bed, or I won't be able to get up and cook our breakfast in the morning."

Her attempt at lightness failed. James reached for her hand, but she headed to her tent. To her retreating back, he asked, "Have you prayed about whether you should marry, or have you already decided for God?" When he saw her body stiffen, he knew he had hit the target for which he'd aimed. As she ducked to enter the tent opening, he said, "I'll continue to pray."

Despite going to bed, Meg could not go to sleep. The question James had asked kept rolling over and over in her mind. She realized she had never prayed about whether she should marry, but then, she'd never had an occasion to wonder about it. The matter suddenly seemed very urgent to her. "Oh, God," she petitioned sincerely, "have I been wrong? Show me your will."

Her last recollection before sleep claimed her was James dousing the fire. He had been up long after she went into her tent. She wondered if he too was praying for her.

Nothing was said about their firelight conversation during breakfast the next morning. James was in a light-hearted mood and dashed from one subject to another.

"I thought we'd go to the Mingo National Wildlife Reserve today. How does that sound?"

"I've never heard of it, but I guess it's okay if you want to go. What is it?"

"About twenty-eight thousand acres of wooded swamps."

"Swamps here in Missouri?" Meg asked in surprise.

"At one time, almost all of Missouri's Bootheel region of two-and-a-half million acres was swamp, but Mingo is the last big tract of this type left in the area."

"But I didn't bring boots, and I don't want to wander through a swamp without boots."

"You won't need them. In the summer the swamp looks more like a dry forest, but in the other seasons, it has water in it. Besides, there's a boardwalk for us to walk. Be sure to grab the insect repellent, though, unless you want the mosquitoes to eat that pretty little nose of yours." James taped her nose lightly as he got up from the table. "Come on, let's get our breakfast mess cleaned up, and then we can leave."

The drive to Mingo took only about twenty minutes and went through rich farming country. Neither said too much; both were engrossed in the other's fascination of the farmers at work. This rural life was so different from the city lives they lived on a daily basis. Meg's hand rested on the seat beside her. When James placed his hand on top of hers, she smiled.

At the entrance to the boardwalk, Meg took a descriptive brochure for the self-guided tour. "If we want to see wildlife, this brochure says we should walk quietly and avoid talking."

"Can we whisper?"

"Sh-h-h-h!"

After walking a few minutes, James reached for the grapevine in front of him and swung over the forest and boardwalk. "When

I was a kid, we'd go to the river in the summer and play on a grapevine for hours. Want to try it?"

Meg repeatedly attempted to swing as far as James had but barely went anywhere.

"I think it's a lost cause," he teased.

"One more time," she pleaded.

One more time was disastrous. As Meg swung over the dried forest, her hand slipped, and she fell into dried leaves. James hopped off the boardwalk to help her, but she was already getting up. "I guess you're right. It's a lost cause."

"You're lucky you didn't break something. Are you okay?"

"My pride is hurt, but otherwise I'm fine."

"I think we just broke the rule about staying on the boardwalk," James said.

"I won't tell if you don't." Back on the boardwalk, Meg continued to read the brochure aloud to James. They learned about the complicated ecosystem that kept wildlife and vegetation functioning properly. At one point they came across a splendid example of poison ivy. "Listen—poison ivy, this brochure tells us, produces small greenish-white berries that wildlife like. I didn't know it did anything besides make me itch."

"Don't move," James spoke quietly. "Do you hear the rat-a-tat-tat? That's a woodpecker." They searched until they spotted him busily looking for insects in a dead tree. "You sure smell good this morning. What kind of perfume are you wearing?"

"Bug spray."

"Let's get out of here," he said as they came to the end of the trail. "When I can't tell bug spray from perfume, I've been in a swamp too long."

James asked Meg if she wanted to walk a trail by the lake. The trail was a pleasant excursion, and they were able to see the dam construction and the outlet channel. It proved an easy walk, as the area was on fairly level ground.

"Let's drive to that concession stand we saw yesterday," James said as they exited the trail.

Meg pointed, "Look at that dog lying right in the middle of the parking lot. I hope he doesn't get hurt."

When they got out of the car, the dog wandered toward them with his head hanging down, his tail tucked between his legs, and his ribs showing. He looked like a beagle mix with his long floppy ears, but his fur was spiky, like he had some type of terrier in him. He was in desperate need of a brushing and bath.

Meg touched James' arm. "He's starving to death. I bet someone has dumped him." She dug through her purse, looking for something to give the dog, and found a partially eaten peanut candy bar. She laid it on the ground, and the dog gobbled it up in just one bite. His tail came up a bit, and he looked at her with hope in his eyes. "I don't have anything else, fella." She looked at James, "Could we buy him something to eat?"

"If we do that, he'll follow us everywhere we go."

"But he's hungry," she pleaded on the starving dog's behalf.

When James ordered three hamburgers, Meg knew she had talked James into having compassion for the starving animal. When they walked to the picnic table, the dog followed and sat beside Meg.

"I am spoiling you, buying a hamburger for a dog." He couldn't believe he'd just purchased one to give to the pathetic looking creature.

"I want to keep him."

"Meg, you can't keep every stray dog you find. You know nothing about him. He could have a bad temperament or a canine disease."

"I don't want every stray dog. I just want this one … please."

James didn't know who looked at him with the most longing— Meg or the stray dog.

Meg was able to get the wiggly, dirty critter on her lap as they headed to their campsite. Several times, the dog gave each of them a happy lick as they drove the short distance to their tents; he seemed to know he had found a home. She guessed James was as concerned about the animal as she was, because he hadn't put up much of an argument against her keeping him.

"Thanks for letting me bring him back to the campsite. I've wanted a dog for a long time, and my landlady has already given me permission to have one. I just couldn't find the right dog until Sadly stole my heart."

"Sadly? Is that what you're going to name the poor creature? What's wrong with Skip or Buster?"

"He looked sad when we first saw him. Names like Skip and Buster are so common. He needs a name that is as unique as he is."

James insisted the dog have a bath so Meg held him as James brought the hose. By the time they finished washing the filthy animal, they were as wet as he was. He had not liked the cold water and had attempted to pull away. Meg's shampoo, however, had done a fairly good job of cleaning him.

"Meg, you and that dog smell alike," James said with a wrinkled nose. "We have to rig up some kind of leash for him to abide by park rules. You also have to clean up his messes."

"I don't have a pooper scooper. Couldn't you do that part?" she questioned in her most innocent voice.

"No, you wanted the dog. With the pleasure comes the responsibility."

"Yuck, I'll hate that part."

"If you find he's more work than you want, we can take him back by the snack shack, and maybe he'll convince someone else to take him home with them."

"I couldn't do that. He likes me," Meg replied.

The fried fish caught the night before was some of the best-tasting fish they had ever had. Sadly lapped up the leftovers but whined because he had to stay on the leash James had fixed for him.

Instead of wandering around the campground that night, they sat around their fire and relaxed. It would be a couple of hours before dark, but the fire was relaxing to watch and helped keep the mosquitoes away. They pulled the picnic table closer to the flames and settled into a game of Scrabble. Since both were competitive by nature, the points scored were essential to winning. They played in silence until Meg's score edged slightly above the points James had achieved.

"I won!" she said triumphantly.

"My ego is crushed. Let's play something else." The evening passed quickly with Monopoly properties sold and won. Sadly had settled close to Meg's feet and occasionally glanced at her with gratitude.

"If you'll fix some hot chocolate, I'll find my Bible and read us a passage before we go to our tents."

Settled back into their lawn chairs, James picked up his New Living Translation Bible. "I'll read Psalm 23," he said and then began. "The Lord is my shepherd; I have everything I need. He lets me rest in green meadows; he leads me beside peaceful streams. He renews my strength. He guides me along right paths, bringing honor to his name. Even though I walk through the dark valley of death, I will not be afraid, for you are close beside me. Your rod and your staff protect and comfort me. You prepare a feast for me in the presence of my enemies. You welcome me as a guest, anointing my head with oil. My cup overflows with blessings. Surely your goodness and unfailing love will pursue me all the days of my life, and I will live in the house of the Lord."

When he finished, Meg asked, "Do you really think God leads our paths in life?"

"Yes, I do. God knows our starts, and He knows our stops. Not one thing that happens to us is ever a surprise to Him."

"What about the bad stuff?"

"Like Amy's death?" he questioned.

"Yeah, how could her death be good? You were hurting so much when you got back from her funeral."

"I don't know all the answers, but I do know God is good. For me, Amy's death was bad, but for her, it wasn't. She's with Jesus. Healing did not come for her during her lifetime, but she is healed with Jesus."

"Some things don't make sense. I just don't see how a loving God can let so much hurt happen."

"When you can't see God's hand, Meg, you've got to trust His heart. God doesn't trust troubles to just anyone. I think He allows troubles to come to make us strong."

"Troubles don't make me strong. They just show what a weak person I am," she said softly.

"Maybe you're trying to handle them yourself without asking for God's help."

For long moments, Meg sat very still staring into the fire. The logs cracked and shot sparks into the night air as the fragrant smoke rose.

"Do you hear the crackle of the wood?" James asked. "It's protesting what's happening to it, but in the end the wood must submit to the fire. Things—good and bad—happen to everyone. We've got to accept them and make the best of them. God didn't tell us everything was good, but he did say if we love him, He'll bring good from everything."

"Maybe"

"Pray about it, and ask God to help you understand. It's not a maybe. It's God's promise."

Meg didn't plan to think about their discussion when she went to her tent, but sleep wouldn't come. Could James be right? Was she trying to handle her problem by herself?

Her prayer was short that night. "Help me, God."

Meg heard James lighting the morning fire but turned over to grab a few more winks. She complained to herself. *No one should wake up at such an ungodly hour when they're camping.* She wadded up her pillow, hit it again, and tried to go back to sleep, but the smell of coffee eventually drove her from her bed. She poked her head out the tent flap, "Can I have a cup of coffee?"

"You look like you could use one," he said when he brought the steaming mug to her. He tousled her uncombed hair making it look even worse. "Sorry I woke you up, but I was awake, so thought I'd get up and watch the morning come to life. No one seems to be stirring in the campground yet but me."

"What time is it?"

"Six o'clock."

"No wonder I feel half dead."

"Go back to sleep. I'll be quiet until the other campers start stirring."

She had settled into her sleeping bag when she remembered she wanted to ask him what time the chapel service began. When she stuck her head out the flap for the second time in as many minutes, she saw James reading his Bible. She didn't want to disturb him, so she lay down and drifted into an easy sleep. ... *James held her in his arms kissing her. "Marry me," he whispered.*

"Oh, yes, my darling. I love you so much."

Sadly's bark awakened her. If only that dream could come true ...

As they walked to the outdoor park where the chapel service was being held, James commented on her unusually good mood.

Smiling brightly, Meg's eyes were sparkling with love as she looked at him.

He wrapped his arms around Meg and gently kissed her. Then he stared at her as though he wanted to memorize every feature of her face "I love you so much. Will you marry me?"

It was as though a bucket of ice water had been thrown on her as her emotions went from hot to cold. She backed away from his arms and wouldn't look at him. Reaching to her chin, he lifted it with one finger. "What's wrong, little one?"

Tears ran down her cheeks. "I can't marry you. I love you, but I just can't marry you. It wouldn't be fair."

"Why, Meg? I know I'm not perfect, and I'll never be rich as a minister in the inner city, but only my relationship with God will come before you. What's not fair?"

"I can't!" She raised her voice loud enough that other park visitors stared at her. "I can't! I just can't!" Meg turned quickly from him and ran back to the campsite. She heard James holler at her to wait. "No!" she yelled back. "Go without me."

Back in her tent, Meg sobbed. Exhausted from her bout of tears, she finally dozed and was lying with her tent flap open when James came back from chapel and found her. Staring at her, he saw her swollen, red eyes, and a wet spot on her pillow.

God, he prayed silently, *I love her and believe you've brought her to me, but she's got a problem bigger than she can handle. Please help her.* He stared at her still-sleeping body and felt love and compassion. If only she would share with him, he was sure they could work out the problem she harbored alone.

"Meg," he said as he patted her shoulder, "it's time to wake up so we can pack. Check out time is 1:00, so we've got work to do."

She opened her eyes and immediately went into his arms. As she snuggled against him, a leftover sob shook her body. "I love you, but I can't marry you. Please understand."

He didn't respond, because he knew she would not reveal her reason. "If you'll pack your things in here first, I'll get us a bite of lunch. My tent is ready to come down, and with your things out, this one will be too. I'll take them down right after we eat.

"You're not mad?"

"It wouldn't do any good to get mad, would it? I love you, but I don't know where to go from here."

As she was packing her things in the tent, she wondered why he wasn't mad. *Well, I can't marry him. Love—who needs it anyway?*

Though he tried several times during lunch to make conversation, Meg barely replied, so he eventually gave up and ate his lunch in silence. He knew she was understandably upset, but since she wouldn't tell him what was wrong, the struggle was between her and God.

Chapter Eight

BACK AT THE resort, Meg was puzzled by James' behavior. He was always polite when they saw one another, but he no longer sought her companionship. In the cafeteria, he found someone else to sit with other than her. But when it was necessary for them to converse with an employee, he included her in the conversation. Several times she stared at him, trying to figure out why he was acting as he did. Eventually, he would notice her looking at him, nod, and smile, but he wouldn't come to her.

"I've had it!" Meg fumed one evening. "I'm going to his cabin right now and find out what's eating him."

A few minutes later, Meg was knocking at his cabin door. There was no answer. She knocked again. When she turned to leave, she saw that Sadly had followed her. "Didn't I tell you to stay home?" she scolded the dog.

"I don't recall your saying that," James said, appearing at the door. "Is there some reason you needed to see me—is everything all right at the store?"

"I was talking to Sadly. He won't stay home."

"Maybe you should have named him Shadow. You can take him to the Humane Society if he's too much bother."

"No."

"Just a suggestion. What did you need?"

He was not going to make this conversation easy for her. She stammered, "I ... I was ... coming ... to ... to talk to you."

"Since you were knocking on my door, I had come to that conclusion."

"May I come in?"

"It would be better if we talked here on the porch."

"I don't want to talk out here. Someone might hear us." Her frustration with him was mounting.

He opened the door for her. "After you."

Meg entered the room but stopped. There was no place to sit until he began removing the stack of books from the only chair in the room.

"I was doing some studying last night and didn't take time to put my stuff away." Clothes were strewn around the room, his bed was unmade, and towels were tossed on the floor.

"Do you live like this all the time?" she asked.

"Don't concern yourself about my room. Now, what did you have on your mind that we need to discuss?"

She could hardly believe this was the same man who just last week had asked her to marry him. "You've acted differently toward me this week."

"In what way?"

"Well," she hesitantly said, "you haven't been around much."

"I've been here all week without a day off."

"You know what I mean!" she exclaimed in exasperation.

"I'm sorry," he sighed. "I know what you mean. But I asked you to marry me, and you turned me down. How do you expect me to act? I'm not going to force you to spend time with me. I thought we had a good thing going, but evidently you don't feel the same. I don't want to waste my time or yours." He looked at her and saw her brows furrow. "Do you want me around?" he questioned.

"Of course I do." She stepped toward him and touched his shoulder.

"Don't, Meg!" he said as he jerked his shoulder away from her.

"I don't know what game you're trying to play, but I'm not playing it. I don't know how to read your actions. One minute you act like you care for me, but the next you don't care that I exist. You're too wishy-washy for me."

Meg knew she was guilty as accused. She had come to talk to him, and she had to do it. "I want to be friends ... that's all."

"That's all!" he shouted. "You know I love you and want to marry you, yet you ask if we can be friends. What do you think I am, Meg?" He took hold of her shoulders. "Look at me! I'm a man—flesh and blood with feelings and desires. I love you!"

His kiss came without warning. So lonely was she for James that she eagerly kissed him in return.

"I love you so much," he mumbled as his lips covered her face with kisses. He rested them on her hair as he held her close. "What am I going to do with you? I don't want to live without you, but you don't want me as your husband."

Her eyes pleaded with him.

"Is friendship all you can give me now?"

She nodded.

"I want you as my wife—my helpmate. I believe with all my heart that you are the woman I've prayed God would send to be my companion for life, but there's still a problem you haven't worked out, isn't there?"

Again, she nodded. As her eyes watered, they spoke volumes.

He had decided the relationship with Meg had no chance of succeeding, but as he saw her hurting, he knew there was hope. It was small, but there was a tiny bit of hope—maybe about the size of a mustard seed.

He walked to the bed and motioned for her to sit beside him. James bowed his head, "Father, You know each of us. You know how much I love Meg. You also know there's a problem she's not willing to share with me. Will you help her as only You know how?" James continued talking to God as though he was talking to his best friend. Meg's heart was breaking. When he finished praying, she was sobbing. "Come on, little one, dry your eyes. You've been in my room too long. I'll walk out with you because we have our reputations to preserve."

Meg and Mattie were enjoying an ice cream cone at the snack shack. "I'm glad to see you and James are friends again. I noticed things were pretty cold between you for a few days. What happened?"

"I don't want to tell you all we discussed, but I'm so glad he's not ignoring me anymore. Until he started doing that, I didn't realize how accustomed I'd become to having him around. I depend on him a lot and really do care about him."

"Look over there," Mattie said, pointing toward the woods. "I've seen him go that way several afternoons now. Why do you suppose he's going to the woods every day? I don't think we've got any campground stuff out there."

"I'll ask him this evening."

"How are Bill and Sherry doing?" Mattie asked changing the subject.

"I'll get to see them when I leave here. I've got a few days before school starts, and I'm going to see my folks. They'll be at Mom and Dad's.

"Are you excited about being an aunt?"

Meg thought for a moment. "I guess I am, but I'm worried too."

"Don't worry about Sherry. She'll be fine. Women have been having babies from the beginning of time. She's healthy and will do great."

"It's not that, Mattie. There's something else that concerns me."

"What could you possibly have to worry about?"

Meg was saved from answering when twin girls walked up and asked for snow cones. While Mattie was serving the customers, Meg slipped away for a walk of her own.

When James came into the general store, Meg asked him about his trips to the woods. Her curiosity rose even more with his strange answer.

"I go out there to talk and to listen." She didn't understand that he was going to pray.

James came into the store and sat in the big wooden rocking chair. "Jan's gotten sick and had to go home. I hate to ask you, but would you clean the rest rooms and showers for me? I'll hold things down here."

"Why, that's just what I've always wanted to do," she said with exaggerated sweetness. "Lead me to the bucket and mop."

"If you'd rather not, I can get one of the other girls to do it. I'd send one of the boys, but I'm afraid they probably don't clean any better that I do. Bert's prided himself on the clean facilities, so I hate to let him down."

"Don't worry, I'll do it, but I'll expect a reward when I'm finished. How about taking me for a burger and fries tonight?"

"If you're treating, it sounds like a great idea," James reasoned.

"If I were treating, I'd cook. Sorry, you're out of luck—you can buy." Meg reached for the bucket and mop. "It's sure good to know I'm going out to eat tonight--maybe fried chicken would be better than a burger and fries."

"Don't press your luck," he laughed as she let the door bang shut.

Meg knocked on the door to the men's room and waited for its occupants to leave before she propped open the door with the trash can. Not wanting to be surprised by an unsuspecting male, she sang as loudly as she could as she scrubbed the shower walls with disinfectant. The chlorine water of the disinfectant was burning her nose and throat so she was anxious to be finished and back into fresh air.

"Nice voice you have, ma'am," a gentleman waiting on the porch said as she removed the trash can from the door. Both laughed, and Meg added, "I didn't want someone to be embarrassed. This isn't my regular job."

She was almost finished with the ladies' room when she spotted the wasp. Hurrying as fast as she could, her fear of the insect accelerated with each swish of the mop. In her rush to get done, she did not spot the second wasp hiding behind the paper towels. When she reached for a towel, the wasp flew directly at her and stung her above her eye.

"James! James!" she screamed as she rushed to the porch.

"What in the world is wrong?" he asked running from the neighboring building.

"A wasp!" she cried. "I might be allergic to the sting." When she raised her hand to the spot, he saw the red, swollen lump. "Stay with me. I'm scared."

"Meg, calm down. You've been stung, and I know it hurts, but there's no reason for panic."

"You don't understand," she wailed. "I stepped on a yellow jacket nest when I was about eleven. I got so many stings that I was really sick and had to stay in bed for three days. I read that one sting can set off the whole reaction again. I'm so scared."

James walked her to the office while attempting to calm her down. Using a soft voice, he told her, "I'm just stepping to the other room to get ice for your eye. I'll be right back and promise I won't leave you. Just to be on the safe side, though, maybe you'd better lie down on Bert's old couch."

He held the ice over the spot as well as he could as he held Meg in his arms to comfort her. "You're going to have quite a shiner there," he teased. "I think you might not want to go anywhere tonight. Some people will sure go to extremes to keep from buying a guy his supper."

Her fear was so strong that she did not even smile at his levity. "Please just hold me. I don't want to die." She didn't have to ask twice.

"You're going to be all right, little one. I'll take care of you." He rocked her back and forth for a long while. He'd been so absorbed in Meg's need to be calmed down and comforted that he had not heard the door to the general store. Chuck was standing in the doorway, grinning sheepishly.

"Sorry, I didn't mean to interrupt," Chuck said.

"She's been stung by a wasp right over her eye, and she's pretty shook up about it."

Seeing Meg's eyes were closed, Chuck quietly walked over to take a peek as James lifted the ice from her eye. "Whoa! That eye is puffed up. I bet it turns black."

"Watch the front desk for me. I'm going to lay her down, but I've got to stay here to watch her in case she has an allergic reaction," he whispered.

Chuck asked the details of the sting after Meg was on the couch.

"Do you have any idea where Bert's first-aid books are?" James asked. "I'll see if I can find out what to expect in case she is allergic to wasp stings. She's drifted off to sleep, and I don't like that so quickly after being stung."

"I'll look for the book. Is there anything else I can do for you?" Chuck asked.

"You can pray for her. And pray that if she needs help, I'll be able to get it for her fast enough."

Chuck located the book and scanned its pages about bee stings. He could find nothing about an allergic reaction of sleeping off a sting. Not knowing what else to do, James stayed close to her until he was convinced her breathing was normal. He quietly rose from his chair, closed his office door, and knelt beside Meg, who was still asleep.

As she began to awaken, Meg heard James talking to someone, but she was too exhausted from her hysteria to move.

"Lord, You know how much I love her, yet I know my love is nothing compared to Your love for Meg. Please, Father, help her be okay from this sting to serve You, whether it's as my wife or not." He began to weep. "Oh, God," he agonized. "she's Yours—not mine. I've tried to claim her as my own, but I give her back to You now to work in her life as You see fit."

Meg, now wide awake, didn't move or open her eyes. She knew James loved her, but had no idea his feelings were so intense. After he rose from kneeling and sat back in the chair for a bit, she spoke. "James."

Instantly he was alert. "Are you okay? You gave me quite a fright, falling asleep after being so scared."

"My eye hurts, but I guess I'm going to live," she said hesitantly.

He reached to touch her swollen eye.

"Ouch … leave it be," she said as she sat up.

"Sorry. I guess it hurts."

"Yes, it does, but I'll be all right in a few days. Am I going to have a black eye?"

He led her to the mirror, "Look for yourself."

It wasn't black, but the eye was definitely swollen. "Oh, I look awful."

"Not to me, you don't. You look better than I've ever seen you." He ever so gently kissed the swollen area.

His kindness lit a fire in Meg. She put her arms around his neck and kissed him.

"M-m-m, very nice," he murmured. "Maybe you should get stung more often."

"How can you say that?" she fired at him.

He laughed. "Just checking to make sure you're okay. I see your sweet disposition is back in place. I've got work to do. You can park yourself in the rocking chair where I can keep an eye on you this afternoon. I'll be taking your place at the counter the remainder of the day."

"I'll do no such thing. I've got to finish cleaning the rest room."

"It's already done. Chuck sent one of his high school buddies to finish it. You're staying right by me this afternoon. That's an order."

Meg knew better than to argue with him once he had made up his mind.

The staff enjoyed teasing Meg the next day, but she insisted on working, saying a swollen eye wouldn't hinder her ability to function. James came in several times to ask her a trivial question. She patiently answered each one, knowing he was checking to make sure she was okay.

Meg's feelings for James had increased dramatically after she heard him praying. Only then had she understood the depth of his love for her. When he released her to the Lord, he had given her the freedom to live her life and make her own choices. She wanted so much to be his wife, but she loved him too much to expect him to live with her when her future looked so bleak. She was deep in thought when James again came in the door with another trivial question.

"What time do I need to pick up the canoes?"

"The same time as always," Meg answered.

"Are you sure the time didn't change?"

"James, I am fine. Would you please stop worrying about me? You've been in every fifteen minutes to check on me."

"You knew why I was coming?"

"Of course, and it is sweet of you to be concerned."

"I'm not worried," he lied. "I know you're in God's hands, but I'm just worried." In two sentences, he had absolutely contradicted himself.

"I am fine. Now get out of here and get your work done."

"Would you be too embarrassed about your eye to go for that hamburger tonight?"

"You're looking at me. What do you think?"

"I think we'll go, but we'll have curb service."

"Is it really that bad?" Meg questioned.

"Let's just say I've seen you looking better."

Later that evening, James drove past the only hamburger joint in town.

"Where are we going?" Meg asked.

"How about Farmington? There are several fast food restaurants there."

"But that's a forty-five-minute drive."

"I guess I'll just get to keep you to myself for a while then."

———

"Look at that guy. He's going to kill himself or somebody else, driving like a maniac. There he goes again." The speeding driver had passed a car on a curve. As the car sped out of sight, James said, "There never seems to be a cop around when you need one."

Several miles down the road, Meg shouted, "Look! That car missed a curve. It's upside down, and I can see the wheels still spinning."

James brought the van to a quick stop, and both ran to the overturned vehicle.

"It's leaking gas and might blow!" James shouted. "Get back!"

Meg ignored James and ran to the passenger side. She heard a groan and then a woman moaning, "My baby ... my baby." Meg grabbed the door handle and miraculously, it opened. She pulled the semiconscious woman from the vehicle and glanced up just long enough to see James pulling the man out. Blood was gushing from his head.

Looking back at the woman, Meg realized for the first time that she was very pregnant. "James, she's having a baby—right now!"

"Pull her back as far from the car as you can. I still think it's going to blow."

He had no sooner spoken than an explosion ripped through the air, knocking both Meg and the woman to the ground. Meg did not move.

"Meg, sweetheart, can you hear me? Please answer me."

Gradually, she opened her eyes and saw him leaning over her. "What happened?" she questioned in total confusion.

"The car exploded. You were closer than I was, so you got knocked down. Can you stand up?" He helped Meg to her feet; she was a bit wobbly but obviously okay. "I need your help. We're about to deliver a baby," he said urgently.

"What?" Meg swayed but James steadied her.

"A passerby saw the car leave the road and has already called an ambulance. They should be here any time, but I don't know if that baby's going to wait. The woman regained consciousness while you were out. She needs you."

James had pulled the pregnant woman farther from the still-burning car, and Meg rushed to her side. Kneeling by the woman, Meg tried to calm her. "My name's Meg. I'm going to be right here with you. Are you going to be able to make it to the hospital?"

"I don't know." She screamed as another contraction hit her. "God, help me!" she begged as still another contraction quickly followed.

"How far apart were your contractions when you left home?"

"Two minutes," she gasped. "Oh, it's coming—the baby's coming!"

Meg heard the siren. "Help's coming. Don't push! James, get them here quick. I can see the baby's head."

The paramedics rushed to the woman and calmly spoke, "Well, it looks like this little fellow is anxious to get here. I guess we'd better help him."

"It's coming! It's coming!" the woman screamed again.

James and Meg stood out of the medic's way as he assisted in the birth. The baby, a perfect little boy, let out a healthy scream as soon as the technician cleared the mucous from his throat. As the man laid the baby at his mother's breast, she asked him if her baby was okay.

"Ma'am, I think any baby who can scream that loud must be all right. He looks fine to me, but we'll have him checked out as soon as we get you both to the hospital. You try to take it easy now."

"Joe—what about Joe? He was afraid we wouldn't make it to the hospital on time. Is he hurt?"

"He's already been taken in the other ambulance while you were delivering your baby. I'm sure the ambulance crew is looking after him."

Meg didn't have the heart to tell her that Joe was unconscious and appeared to be seriously hurt. She prayed he'd recover from his injuries and that this young family could go on with their lives.

After the ambulance left with mother and baby, James and Meg told the officers what they had seen before the accident.

"Too bad," the policeman replied. "I hope the guy makes it. With head wounds, you never know. He was so scared that he didn't use common sense. He could have killed his wife and baby."

Back in the car, James and Meg looked at one another and then at their clothes. "It's a good thing we weren't planning on a fine restaurant," James said. "Between the explosion and their injuries, we're filthy."

"Honestly, James, I don't think I could eat a thing. Could we go to the hospital and check on the couple?"

"Do you suppose they'll let us in with this filth on us?"

"We can wash up in the restrooms, and if anything is said about our clothes, we'll explain that we were at the accident scene."

At the hospital, they stayed just long enough to learn that Ellen Miles, the young mother, and her baby were doing fine. Ellen only had a few bruises. She had been cleaned up and her baby had been brought to her.

Joe Miles, however, was listed in critical condition. If he made it through the night, he might have a chance for survival.

———

James and Meg returned to the hospital the next day and were allowed to visit Ellen. "Our baby's fine," she said with relief. "He doesn't have a mark on him. Thanks so much for what you did." Then she added, "Joe's not doing well. They don't know if he's going to make it. They won't even let me go see him," she cried.

Meg sat on her bed and hugged the upset woman. So much had happened to this young woman in a short period.

When Ellen again was under control, James spoke. "I don't know what the future holds for Joe, you, and the baby, but I know Someone who does. Let's ask God to spare Joe's life." James bowed his head and said, "Lord, we acknowledge You as the giver of life. We know You put these bodies together, and we're asking You to put Joe together again. Repair his body and make him well. Help him to be able to come to Ellen again as a loving husband, and let him be a good father to his son. We ask Your wisdom for the doctors as they minister to him and ask that You sustain Ellen during this time of waiting."

After talking with Ellen a little longer, they left. When they reached the elevator, a man with a chaplain's badge stepped out as the door opened. When Meg started to step inside, James held her back. "Wait—I want to see which room he enters."

They saw him enter Ellen's room and looked at one another with deep sadness. Then they heard her scream, "No! My Joe can't be dead! We've got a new baby!"

Meg turned ashen.

"Are you going to be all right?" James asked. As she nodded, James said, "We've got to go to Ellen. She needs us, but if you can't do it, I'll go alone. Joe was dead before I prayed."

They entered the room to find a distraught Ellen sobbing uncontrollably. For the second time within just a few minutes, Meg gathered the young mother, now a new widow, in her arms and held her as she wept bitter tears of grief.

After a few minutes, the chaplain left, and James and Meg were alone with her. They each prayed within their hearts that God would give them words of comfort for the young woman. It was their presence and not their words, however, that brought the most comfort.

As they talked, a nurse entered to administer a sedative to Ellen. "I don't want a sedative," she cried. "I just want my Joe."

"We'll be back when the nurse leaves," James said.

As the nurse left, she told James and Meg they would only have about ten minutes before the sedative took effect. "It's such a shame--a fine new baby and no husband to share the joy. I'll never understand why these things happen."

Nor I, thought Meg. *How can God be so cruel?*

~~~~~~~

"I could use a cup of coffee. How about you?" James asked as they left Ellen's room.

In the hospital snack bar, James and Meg sat quietly.

"I don't understand why Joe died," Meg confessed. "Why did God take Joe when He knows Ellen and the baby need him? It's so unfair." She stared at the coffee as though it had mesmerized her.

James didn't deny Meg's words. In fact, he was thinking how many times he had asked that same question—why? If only there was a simple explanation.

"I'm asking *you* why," Meg said. "Just tell me one good reason God had for taking Joe. How can God leave a young widow with a newborn baby and call it good? Doesn't the Bible say everything is good?"

"No, it doesn't, but it says something similar. The Bible says God works everything for good to those who love Him. There is a big difference between everything being good and everything working for good. We both know not everything is good, but God promises to bring good from even bad things when we love Him. We know of horrible things—car crashes like Joe and Ellen's, murders, rapes, robberies. They're not good, but God can bring good from them."

James took a sip of coffee and then continued. "I read once about a couple whose daughter had been brutally raped and murdered. The grief-stricken parents wanted to meet the man and rage at him for what he had done to their daughter. When they met him, however, instead of hating him, God gave them compassion for this young man whose life was also now ruined. They decided they couldn't bring their daughter back, but they could minister to her murderer and rapist. Their concern for him eventually led to his accepting Christ as his Savior. Today, he is out of prison and a welcome guest in their home."

"I couldn't forgive like that. How could they forgive her killer and welcome him to their home? That's absurd."

"Don't you see, Meg, we can't, but the Spirit of God who lives in us can give us the heart to do that. God loves us. It's true most of us don't have to go to the extent this couple did, but if you think about it, you'll see some instances where God did bring good out of bad."

"The McIntyre's adopted a little boy from Honduras when they couldn't have children," she said.

"Exactly. I imagine their hearts were broken when they learned they couldn't have children, but God opened their hearts to love a child who needed love. He allowed that child to become their own son. Whatever happens in our lives, even our sins and mistakes, He can turn into good when we love Him. God promised that in Romans 8:28, and God always keeps His promises."

"Maybe you're right, but I still have trouble understanding it."

"God wants our complete trust, not partial trust. Try sometime turning something you think is bad over to God. You'll discover God will bring good from it. Remember, though, that His ways and our ways are never the same. We cannot guess what God will do."

Meg suddenly got out of her chair. "Are you ready to go? I've had about all the goodness of God I can stand for one day," she stated bitterly.

Meg's bitterness toward God cut into his heart. *I think she's talking about more than Joe and Ellen*, James thought. *She's holding a grudge against God about something, but I don't know what it is.*

Chapter Nine

$\mathcal{M}$EG BECAME QUIET and restless after the hospital visit. James did his best to get her to talk about what was bothering her, but she became more sullen and depressed as the days went by. She was barely eating and her clothes started to hang on her.

She made several visits to see Ellen after she went home from the hospital. All she wanted to talk about was Ellen's situation. She withdrew from James and didn't laugh anymore.

One morning she went to see James in his office. "I'm leaving a week early. I've got some things I need to do before school starts."

"You must be eager to get back to your students," he offered.

"Not particularly. I'm going to help Ellen. She doesn't have any family near, and she needs help sorting out her finances and deciding what she's going to do now."

"If there's some way I can help her, will you let me know?"

With her promise to do so hanging in the air, Meg prepared to leave River's View at the end of her work day. *What can I tell Ellen?* she wondered, *"Hey, cheer up. God is good. That's why you feel like you're dying inside. You're a young widow, have a new baby, no job, and a lot of bills. Yes, everything is great and wonderful."*

Meg left the next morning without a good-bye to James. Sadly sat beside her staring out the window.

At Ellen's home, she was greeted by a much-relieved young widow. "Thanks so much for coming, Meg. It means a lot to me that you'd care enough about a stranger you met on the road to come stay with me. You have been such a help to me already."

"How are you doing?"

"Okay," Ellen assured her.

"Now you've given the polite answer, I want to know how you're really doing."

Ellen shrugged. "I cry every day. The baby won't sleep at night, I'm exhausted, and I've so much to figure out about the future that I'm overwhelmed. More than anything, I want my Joe back. I wish we could have all died together. It would have been so much easier."

"I don't know why, but you are alive. You've got a fine, healthy young son to nurture, and he's depending on you because you're all he has. I'm going to help you this week, and maybe by the end of my time here, you'll be feeling more like yourself and be able to decide what you should do next. Right now, I'll watch little Joey so you can go rest."

Meg had forced an enthusiasm and confidence in God she didn't feel. "Go on with you now. When you get rested, things will look a lot brighter. By the way, I brought my dog with me. Is there somewhere I can keep him?"

"Bring him in the house. It'll be nice to have a four-legged friend inside."

Meg went with Ellen to the bedroom and tucked a sheet around her. "I know things are really hard, and you're going to hurt for a long time. But you are stronger than you think you are, and you will survive. God will help you, and I will help. You are going to make it through this crisis."

"Okay, Meg. You are so encouraging. Take care of Joey for me. I just want to rest"

Meg had started a load of laundry when little Joey let her know he was ready for a feeding and diaper change. *That child certainly has good lungs!*

Oh, great, Meg pondered. *I didn't ask about his bottles.* To her relief, when she went to the refrigerator, bottles were prepared. She warmed one with hot water and offered it to the infant.

Joey, satisfied to be full and dry, smiled at Meg. *Probably a gas pain,* she reasoned, but his little smile had warmed her heart anyway. She was so sorry the little guy would never know his daddy. From the little she had learned about Joe from Ellen, he sounded like a great guy. She cuddled the baby to her while thoughts of James filled her imagination. *James was holding their baby, changing their baby's diaper, and then playing horsey with a toddler.*

Why am I daydreaming? Meg thought angrily. *It can never be. I might as well break if off with him now.* She just couldn't think of a way to do it, not realizing it was because she didn't want to lose his love. Sadly laid his head on her leg and whined.

She was preparing dinner when a much-rested Ellen appeared in the doorway.

"It smells good in here. What are you fixing?"

"Tuna casserole. It's my standby when I don't know what else to fix," Meg responded.

"I'm famished since I slept through lunch."

"You needed to rest. Are you feeling a bit better?"

Ellen assured her she was.

"I have things under control. The laundry's done, the house is straightened, and Joey's asleep. He smiled at me after I fed him, and my heart melted. Dinner will be ready in about ten minutes, but you have time to freshen up a bit if it will make you feel better."

Meg was humming to herself when the doorbell sounded bringing Sadly to his feet with loud barking.

"Hi," James said, grinning at Meg and reaching to pet the dog. "Am I in time for supper? I brought groceries to help Ellen. Take this bag, and I'll get the other two." He handed Meg the sack and turned back to the car.

The conversation was relaxed as they were eating, until Joey cried. Meg rose to get him, but Ellen was faster. "You've worked all day. It's my turn."

"How's she doing?" James asked after Ellen had left the room to get the crying infant.

"A day's sleep helped. She's really lonesome, but I guess that's to be expected. She was exhausted when I got here."

"You look more relaxed than you did at the resort. What have you done all day?" When Meg told him, he grinned. "It sounds to me like you needed some hard work to cheer you. I must not have given you enough to do."

"Joe's death has been eating at me. I just can't understand why God would let him die when Ellen needs him so much. I know you've heard me say that before, but it just doesn't make sense to me."

James cautiously replied, "There are a lot of things that don't make sense to us. It's like we're under an umbrella. We can't see anything except the inside of the umbrella, but God is over the umbrella and sees the big picture. God doesn't tell us why things happen. He wants us to trust that He is in control."

"So I live under the umbrella. I can't see what God sees. Tell me why God allows Ellen to suffer. Why does He mess up people's lives? Why doesn't He stop evil? Answer those questions, and I'll be happy under my umbrella."

"We'll talk later," he whispered as Ellen came into the room with her baby. "Can I hold that big boy?"

Joey was still crying as James lifted him to his shoulder and gently patted his back. Within a minute, the fretful baby stopped crying. Meg turned her head away from the scene. It was too perfect—too much like her daydreaming had been earlier in the day.

Ellen took little Joey and fed her young son the bottle she'd warmed then handed him back to James. At Ellen's first yawn, Meg again sent her off to bed. "I'll watch the baby. Are there enough bottles to last through the night?"

"I've slept all day," Ellen protested. "If I go to bed, though, you and James can talk. Give him a kiss for me. I'd give anything to be able to kiss Joe." With sagging shoulders, she left the room. Even though she closed her bedroom door, James and Meg thought they could hear crying.

Meg lay Joey in his crib and came back to snuggle into James' arms. "I like it here," she said. "I expected you to come but not the first day I got here." His arms cuddled her, and she felt totally at home and at peace until Sadly pushed his nose between the two of them.

"I missed you today, little one. If only you knew how much I love you." Meg had heard James say that so many times that she had become used to hearing it. When he kissed her, it was full of emotion. "Oh, Meg, I love you so much."

She kissed him back and grinned impishly. "That's for Ellen. You heard her tell me to kiss you for her since she can't kiss Joe."

He reached toward her again for another kiss, but she didn't cooperate. "Don't press your luck, buddy. Enough is enough, and we'd better be good."

"You're right, but I don't want to stop." Instead, he changed the subject. "So, how did you like playing homemaker and mommy today?"

"It was great. Joey's such a sweet little guy. It's so sad that his daddy never got to meet him."

"Maybe someday Ellen will marry again, after she's had time to heal. It would be nice if she would, and the guy could be Joey's new daddy."

"How long does it take to stop hurting?"

"Psychologists say at least a couple of years."

"Why, James?"

"It just takes that long to get over the death of a loved one."

"No, that's not what I meant. I want to know why God took Joe."

"It seems to me that Joe died because he was driving carelessly, trying to get Ellen to the hospital. He meant well, but he took unnecessary chances, and it cost him his life. God didn't zap him and say 'Gotcha.' We both saw how he was driving. When people do stupid things, they pay the consequences."

"Ellen needed to get to the hospital," Meg insisted.

"Sure she did, but other men don't drive like that to get their wives to the hospital. Very few babies are born along the roadways, because the majority of them make it."

"Are you saying God didn't have anything to do with Joe's dying—it was actually his fault? God could have made Joe drive more carefully."

"That's not the way God operates. We're not puppets. God gives us choices and sets things in order. When we break the natural laws God has set up, we pay the penalty. Joe didn't control his vehicle and paid for it with his life. It's as simple as that."

"And now Ellen is left alone and hurting," she countered. "It's just not fair."

"Others often suffer the consequences of someone else's actions."

During Meg's week at Ellen's, James visited two more evenings.

"I miss you at River's View, but I'm glad you came. Ellen needed you more than the resort, and both of you seem to be doing better. I was getting worried about you."

"Hopefully, I've helped her get over the first big hump. I've prayed a lot for her too and feel like she will be able to make it now. When she is able to get a job and finds a good babysitter, she'll be okay. Time heals, I've heard, so I guess now what she needs is time. I'm leaving Saturday to go back to St. Louis. My summer has been great, and I appreciate so much your being my friend this summer. I needed one."

"Meg ..." James began, beginning to get agitated.

"Don't say anything. I told you all I could offer was friendship. Now I'm going home with happy memories of the time we've enjoyed being together. I'll always cherish this summer as a very special time in my life."

The usually controlled James lost his temper. "Is that all—something special? I have told you over and over that I love you, and you act like it's no big deal. '*So long, buddy, it's been nice knowing you. Now go back to your books. I don't care. Just get out of my life.'* Is that what you're saying? *'Get lost, James'?"*

Meg was at a total loss for words, but James wasn't. "All you care about is what you want, Meg. You're not the only person in the world who has plans." He took a deep breath, fighting for control. "I love you, Meg. Does my love mean nothing to you?"

She stood immobilized staring at the floor. He gazed long and silently at her, but when she didn't reply, he turned and left the room. The door quietly shut behind him as he said, "Don't ever forget that I love you."

Meg had done what she had to do. She loved James enough to send him away. He would never know she loved him with all her heart. From the depth of her being, she felt as though her heart was crushed, and she would never recover.

September was hot and muggy, something not at all unusual for St. Louis. Meg was glad to be back in school with her students and busy schedule. Each day, she'd go to her mailbox, hoping to see a letter from James. Her phone was silent. Only in her memory could she hear, "I love you, Meg." Her heart was aching, and her sleep was restless. She knew she was not giving her all to her students because her heart had been left with James. Only Sadly was there for her to hug.

Evidently, James had taken her at her word, since she had not heard from him. The summer's relationship was over, just as she told him she wanted it to be. In the past, he had sought to reconcile any differences. This time he did not.

In order to keep from going a little berserk, Meg got active in school activities and her church's Sunday School class for singles. The busy life she had did not stop the void she felt when she was alone. Only one person would fill that void, and she would not contact him.

After a month of longing for James, she decided a change of scenery would help. She took a personal day from school to spend a three-day weekend with her parents. Meg hoped that being around them would help her put her life back into perspective, so she could go on with her life.

Meg and Sadly traveled the interstate to her parents' mid-state home—it was a quicker route than the scenic two-lane route. Although bored with the monotony of the road, driving on I-44 left her plenty of time to think. That wasn't good, however, because she wanted to avoid thinking—her thoughts always went to one person. She drifted back to the first float trip with James and the kiss he'd given her. Things about the summer ran through her mind like a recording—James' kindness when she was stung by the wasp, his mischievousness when he threw her in the river, his struggle with grief when Amy died. She knew she would do anything for James that he asked her to do—except marry him. She would not burden him with marriage for the rest of his life. She knew him well enough to know that if they married, it would be forever. How she wished things had been different. Her old concern about the unfairness of life again rose to haunt her.

Mitchell Green saw his daughter's car coming down the tree-lined drive. "Mama, she's coming. Come, so we can greet our baby."

Hugs and kisses flowed freely almost before Meg could get out of the car. They were a balm to her injured soul. Sadly jumped from the car and immediately spotted a rabbit to chase.

"Dad, that bear hug would squeeze a grizzly to death," Meg teased.

"Gosh, girl, I have to make up for lost time. We haven't seen you for a while … but I'm not complaining 'cause you're here now."

The three settled on the screened-in back porch. Mitchell and Meg sat on the porch swing, while Sarah, her mother, sat across from them. Mitchell had his arm around his only daughter.

"Tell us about this summer at River's View. Usually, we hear from you a lot when you're there, but this summer you must have been too busy to call or write. You didn't show up here the week before school either."

"I'm sorry I didn't contact you more often. I was pretty busy. Remember I told you that Bert broke his back and his friend James was taking his place? Things weren't the same with Bert not there. James and I did float a couple of times. We made trips to see Bert. The rest of the time, I worked. That's about all I did—except we got to see a baby born. That was quite an experience!"

"Tell us about the baby."

She related the story to her parents who sympathized with the newly widowed Ellen.

"I notice you keep saying 'James and I,'" Mitchell teased. "Maybe we want to hear a lot more about this new boyfriend."

She grinned because her daddy knew her too well. "Boyfriend?" she responded nonchalantly.

"Tell us more, because we need a son-in-law. Maybe we can talk him into marrying you."

Meg wouldn't look at them. Mitchell had not gotten the answer to his question about James, but he would wait; he would get his answer from his daughter.

Meg turned to her mother, saying brightly, "Mom, you look good. How have you been?"

"Some good days, some bad. You know how it is with me. I couldn't survive without your dad."

Mitchell smiled at his wife. "I wouldn't be happy without you, so I'm glad to help when I can. It doesn't seem to me like you need much help." Meg could see that their love was as strong as it had ever been, and she savored the wonderful memories she had of their continual romance.

Still, Meg sat silently and pondered. *How could her dad say what he did? He's been tied down to Mom for years*, she thought. *Anything he wants to do takes twice as long. He even does most of the housework.*

Meg smiled and asked, "What's for supper?"

"Grilled hamburgers. Dad knows that's your favorite grilled food. I made Jell-O salad and cheesecake too. I thought I'd let you fry some potatoes. I've got them peeled and soaking in water."

Supper was a cheerful occasion. Meg caught up on all the local news from her parents, who delighted in telling her the details.

She learned that most of her college friends were married, but her high school sweetheart was still single.

Mitchell prodded her with more questions about James. She reluctantly answered, but her comments were as brief as possible. She had made this trip so she could think about something and someone other than James. She couldn't do that when her dad kept asking questions about him.

After dinner, Mitchell and Meg cleaned the table that sat close to the open window. The smell of grilled burgers still permeated the air. "Can I have hamburgers for every meal while I'm home?" Meg asked.

"It would be okay with me, but I'm afraid your mother is going to insist you have well-balanced fare. She'll tell you to eat a variety of things, so you get all your vitamins and keep some meat on those bones. It looks to me like you've lost some weight. You're not sick, are you?"

Meg didn't answer but carried the dishes to the sink. Mitchell watched her from the corner of his eye. He saw sadness reflected on her face, but he remained silent. Something was bothering his daughter, but he needed time to pray and think about it. He asked his heavenly Father for wisdom before talking with her. Something was bothering Meg, and he had a sneaky feeling that something was a *someone* named James.

Sarah went to bed early, as was her custom. It took Mitchell a few minutes to get her out of the wheelchair, bathed, and in bed.

"I smell popcorn. I'll fix lemonade to go with it, and then we can go out to the porch swing," Mitchell said after returning to Meg.

Popcorn and lemonade was a Green family favorite snack and had been all Meg's growing-up years. As Meg treasured another taste of home, she and her dad chatted freely. At last he asked, "Tell me, daughter—what's bothering you?"

"Nothing, Daddy," she lied as she reached to pet her dog.

Mitchell put his arm around her shoulders. "Meg, you've never held anything from me. Why start now? Your dad still has a listening ear, and I might actually be able to help." He gave his daughter time to speak but didn't press her. He knew she'd talk when she was ready and not before. He felt her shudder as she quickly turned and buried her face on his shoulder.

"It's James, Daddy," Meg finally said. "I'm so lonesome for him. He hasn't written, called, or come to visit since I've been back in St. Louis."

"Why not? Can't he see my daughter's the best female around?"

"I told him our summer friendship had been nice, and I'd always remember it as something special. Not once did I tell him that I love him, but I do."

"You've lost me. Why did you tell him the summer had been just nice if you love him? You must be head-over-heels in love with him to have this kind of reaction."

"Because of Mama."

"You're going to have to explain what you mean. I can't see what your Mama has to do with you and James, since she's never even met him."

"Because I won't put James through what you've had to experience with Mama. I refuse to saddle him with a cripple!"

"Hey, just you wait a minute. Let's get something straight. I am not 'saddled,' as you put it, to your Mama. I love her, and everything I do for her is because of that love. Sure, she's in a wheelchair. So what? That doesn't make me love her any less. It just gives me a chance to show her how much I love her by helping her when she needs it."

"She's kept you from doing all kinds of stuff, Daddy, and you know she has."

"We couldn't do some things, but think for a minute. Have you ever once heard me complain about not being able to do something?"

"No, but—"

"Because I want to be with her. Only my relationship with God is more important than the one I share with your mama. Besides, what's that got to do with you and James?"

"You know I have a 50-50 chance of inheriting her illness. I won't put James through what you've been through, even if you say it is your privilege to help her!" She was as adamant as she'd been a bit earlier.

"Have you asked James his feelings? You don't have the right to make this decision for him."

"I have every right, when I'm the one who might be the burden!" Meg said hotly.

"So you're smarter than both James and God, are you? You've decided you're getting the disease. You've decided you can't marry. You've decided to make yourself and James miserable if he loves you like you think he does. Where's the faith I've tried to teach you? All your life, we've attempted to teach you to trust God, but it seems to me like you've deserted Him."

"I have not!" Meg countered. "I go to church every Sunday."

"Anybody can go to church. What do you have when you come out those church doors? If your faith can't carry you through the tough times, then you've got no faith at all. You'd better go to bed and think about what I've said." Mitchell hugged his daughter. "I've been hard on you, but you're wrong on this one, honey. Somebody had to tell you, and it looks like I was elected. Now get yourself to bed."

Meg pleaded, "Daddy, please understand."

"This time it's not your earthly father you need—it's your heavenly Father. I would do anything for you, but God will give you His best if you let Him be in control. You've got to decide who's going to be in charge of your life? Whom are you going to trust?"

Meg rose from the swing and started toward her room.

"Remember, I love your Mama. She's God special gift to me."

Meg did not comment, but she heard what he said. Her battle lasted until the wee hours of the morning. Meg's Bible was in her lap. Its words penetrated her heart. "My grace is all you need; power comes to its full strength in weakness." (2 Cor. 12:9 NEB)

At long last, she finally said, "Okay, God, I give up my right to myself. I'm letting You take over. Please guide me. If I get Mom's disease, would You help me use even that to bring honor to You?" She continued her prayer. "I've really made a mess of things with James, too. If You want us to be together, would You work it so we can be together as man and wife? If I'm to stay single, would

You make the ache in my heart go away? And please help James--I know he's hurting like I am."

With the peace only God could give, Meg finally slept.

<div align="center">~~~~~~~~</div>

Sadly took his place on the front seat as Meg hugged her parents good-bye and thanked them for putting up with her over the weekend.

"Don't you know the greatest gift you can give your parents is your presence? We love to have you come back here," Mama said. "Do so as often as you can."

Meg went home, anticipating she would hear from James since she had turned the situation over to God, but the communication lines stayed silent. However, she discovered a contentment she had not known previously.

She was so grateful God had given her a dad who challenged her wrong thinking. She did the same school and church activities, but now she enjoyed them. She had told God He was in charge of her life, so she did everything as if she was doing it for Jesus, but still she did not hear from James.

Fall slipped into the holiday season. A pulmonary virus was going around the school, and she got it. For days, she coughed, even after seeing a doctor. At times, she thought she would cough her lungs out of her chest. She missed an entire week of school, but she used it wisely. When she wasn't coughing or resting from the fatigue brought on by the virus, she had her Bible in her hand. She had developed a hunger for the Word of God that could not be satisfied. The more she learned, the more she wanted to learn.

Every day she prayed for herself and James. Every day things stayed the same. Meg wondered if God was going to have her stay single, as she had said earlier she wanted to do. Whatever happened, she was content. God was in control.

Just before Thanksgiving, Meg received a letter from Ellen. She had moved closer to her parents, and her mom was babysitting little Joey while Ellen worked as a waitress. She said she still missed Joe, but the hurt wasn't quite as bad as it had been. Sometimes she could go two or three days without crying. A young man had come into the restaurant and was paying a lot of attention to her, but she felt it was too soon to encourage him. Maybe someday she would but not yet.

Even Bert had written, thanking her for the fine job the staff did at the resort during the summer. He said he was able to move around but wasn't up to speed yet. He was doing a few chores, but he was leaving the heavy work to the winter crew. He was glad she and James were dating, since they were his favorite two resort workers.

Meg realized that Bert was misinformed, but he meant well. She would not correct him until she saw him next summer. He had asked her to come back to the resort again. That was an answer to a prayer. Maybe James would be there, and she could tell him how sorry she was for the mess she had made of their relationship. She hoped he would forgive her and welcome her back. She knew she had hurt him, however, and didn't know if he would or could forgive her.

Chapter Ten

*J*AMES LOOKED OVER the list of churches requesting names of potential pastoral candidates among seminary graduates. He saw church locations in several states but guessed it didn't make one bit of difference which way God wanted him to go, since he had no family.

He wanted to serve wherever he was called, but more than anything, he wanted to continue to prepare for the inner-city ministry to which God had called him. During his seminary days, he had been able to do quite a bit of volunteer work at a homeless shelter and a juvenile home for boys in the inner city. His heart went out to the boys. Most had grown up with no father figure in their lives.

At the homeless shelter, he saw teen couples living together who shared a child but had not yet reached adulthood themselves. They had no one to whom they could turn and so relied on each other for support. A fire at the old hotel that was run as the homeless shelter sent many of them back into the streets until the needed repairs could be made. He could not help but wonder how many of them he would see again.

He had tried to forget Meg by having no communication with her. He did not call or write, but he wished he knew how she was doing. He did his best to put her out of his mind, but he was not successful. Every day she invaded his thoughts, but nights were worse, as he dreamed about her. It had been over three months since he had seen her, but she was as much in his thoughts as she was at the resort.

James looked over the list of churches again. Since Missouri was his home state and the area he knew best, he sent a résumé to each potential church. He hoped to be near enough to Kansas City to occasionally check at the homeless shelter and juvenile home. He had begun making a little progress with some of the teens and didn't want to lose the connection he had with them, if they stayed around long enough.

Once the résumés were in the mail, he settled into his studies and left the choice of a place to serve to God.

He was invited to preach the Sunday sermon at several of the churches. Grace Church he especially liked and felt they also liked him. After much prayer, both the congregation's and his own, he was asked to be their pastor. The people in the church were friendly and kind; he got to know them and some of the members had spiritual depth, while others needed a lot of growth. An abundance of teenagers especially pleased him, as he would get valuable experience for working with the inner-city kids.

James found an apartment and moved to the area the weekend before Christmas. He was now a seminary graduate and ready to serve beginning the first week in January.

James looked at his new congregation the first Sunday in the pulpit. They were well-balanced in age. He could see older folks whom he hoped would have wisdom and younger ones who already showed enthusiasm to try new things. "Teach Us Your Way, O Lord" was his first sermon as pastor.

After the service, he received several invitations to Sunday dinner. Although he accepted the first one, he took rain checks for the others. He sure didn't want to miss a meal, because he did not like his own cooking.

Mitchell Green, the first to ask him that Sunday, turned to his new pastor. "Brother James, you can just follow my van home. Mama and I aren't fancy, but we're looking forward to getting to know you as you share our table. I think you'll find our food edible." He patted the young pastor on his back.

James watched the back of the blue van as it traveled the country roads around one turn after another. He was glad he was following instead of having instructions to get there. The van stopped in front of a modest home that had an attractive and welcoming yard.

James watched as Mrs. Green maneuvered her wheelchair from the specially equipped van. "May I help?" he offered.

"Goodness no," Mitchell said. "We've done this for so long we can get this wheelchair out with our eyes closed. Me and Mama have our routine set and know just what the other is going to do."

Obviously not at all bothered by the chair, the couple led James up the ramp to their home.

"Have a seat, Preacher. Dinner will be ready in a few minutes if you want to sit and watch us. Or you can take off your necktie and come help us."

"That sounds like the best idea to me," James said. He pulled off his tie and rolled up his sleeves as he sauntered into the kitchen, totally fascinated by the couple. They were obviously happy and comfortable with one another. Whatever had caused Mrs. Green to be in a wheelchair had evidently been totally accepted.

James set the table and carried bowls of food to the table. Mrs. Green wheeled her chair to the setting that had no chair behind it. They joined hands, and his host and hostess smiled their private looks at one another. "Let us pray," Mitchell said. "Father, we thank You for this food so lovingly prepared by Mama. Give our bodies strength from it. Now Lord, we also want to thank You for sending us our new pastor. He's young and needs your wisdom as he guides our church. You know we're a stubborn bunch of folks sometimes, so he's going to need lots of help from You. Help Mama and me to always support the man when he speaks for You, and we're expecting to hear from You a lot. Help us sheep not to wander away from our shepherd."

"Thanks so much for that prayer," James said, looking directly at Mitchell. "It makes me feel welcome. Please continue to pray for me, too. I surely need it when ..."

As he spoke, his eyes had drifted to a small picture on the hutch. He stopped mid-sentence and stared.

Mitchell followed the direction of James' look. It was Meg's picture he was studying. James looked as if he had seen a ghost. Could this be the James Meg loved? Mitchell laughed silently. *Now wouldn't that be just like the Lord to send James right to our doorstep?* Mitchell decided to wait to ask questions.

James continued to stare at the photo until he eventually sighed and began to eat. Whatever he was going to say earlier was left unsaid. Instead, he asked, "Are you Meg Green's parents?"

Sarah Green smiled at her new pastor. "Why, yes. How did you know? She's our pride and joy, but we don't get to see her as much as we'd like. She's got her own life now."

"I met her this summer at River's View Resort. She's a fine young woman, and you have every right to be proud." James shared with Meg's parents some of the events of the summer. They were especially interested in hearing about Bill and Sherry's visit and more about the accident that resulted in Meg's help to the young widow.

Mitchell noticed that the longer James talked about Meg, the more enthusiastic he became in his praise of her. However, he made no reference to his love for her.

"Does Meg know you're our new pastor?" Mitchell asked.

"Not unless you've told her. We haven't been in touch since we left the resort. Meg thought it would be better if we didn't ..." Again, he stopped speaking in mid-sentence and asked instead, "Does she come home often?"

"Usually she makes it for Christmas, but she called the other day to say she wouldn't be able to come. Christmas afternoon, she went with a bunch of girls to a convention. She'll probably come for Easter this year," Sarah said hopefully.

"Would you not tell her I'm here?" James asked.

"Well, forever more! And why would we not want her to know that her friend is our new pastor? I really think she'd want to know," Sarah insisted.

"Sarah, now let's do what James has asked. I think he has his reasons." Mitchell looked at James and winked.

Mitchell knows I love her, James thought. *But how could he know? Is it possible Meg told him?* In his heart, hope soared like an eagle about to climb the heights. Maybe he should write her. No, maybe he should call her. No, she might hang up on him. He'd just have to wait. Easter would be a long time to wait, but he could do it. It would give him a lot more time to pray.

After dinner, the three sat in the living room before the fireplace and discussed the future of the church. James could see Sarah was getting tired, so decided it was time for him to leave.

Mitchell walked with him to his car. As James reached for the door handle, Mitchell laid his hand on James' shoulder. "You love our Meg, don't you?"

James turned and looked directly into Mitchell's eyes. "Yes, sir, I do. She's the finest woman I've ever met. I asked her to be my wife, but she turned me down."

"I think we need to talk. Let's walk toward the pond. Mama will take a nap. She expects me to be out a while so it's no problem."

James did not hesitate. He told Mitchell everything. It was evident that he was deeply in love with Mitchell's daughter. "She says friendship is all she can give me. When we left the resort, she said the summer would be some of her best memories. Sir, I'm not proud of this, but I got mad. I told her I loved her, and she threw that love back at me. I can't be just a friend with her. I want her for my wife, and I still believe God sent her to me. She's got some kind of a problem but wouldn't share with me what it was or why she wouldn't get married. She kept saying she couldn't marry."

"Keep talking, son. I think I know her problem."

"Sir, I'm trying hard to go on with my life, but I can't stop thinking about her. I love her with all my heart."

"The problem is Mama," Mitchell inserted into the conversation.

"What do you mean? Your wife had never met me until I came

to preach at your church. Why would she object to my marrying your daughter?"

"Mama doesn't even know you love our Meg. Let's sit down on this log, and I'll tell you about Meg and Mama." They seated themselves with their legs stretched in front of them. "Meg has a 50-50 chance of inheriting Mama's illness. We talked about you, and she told me she loved you, but also emphatically said she would not saddle you with a cripple and tie you down like Mama has tied me down. Oh, boy, did we have a discussion then! I informed her in no uncertain terms that I loved Mama with all my heart and was not tied down. Then I told her I'd rather be with Mama than out doing other things. I got pretty upset with her, believe you me, and I told her she should ask you and God about it instead of deciding things for herself."

"Do you mean she won't marry me because she's afraid she'll get the illness that has crippled Mrs. Green?"

"Slow down, son. Let me tell you all about Meg's visit a while after school started." He took his time but told James what had happened. "I knew Meg was really unhappy. Oh, she tried to fake it, but a daddy knows when one of his kids isn't happy. It didn't take me long to put two and two together. I figured out the James she mentioned several times was at the heart of the problem. It took me a while, but I somehow got it out of her. I was pretty tough on her. She said you got mad at her when she broke things off with you. I did worse than that—I let her have it with both barrels, if you know what I mean. I told her I'd rather have Mama crippled than have any other woman on this earth. I think it shocked her, because she sure acted surprised. Then I got really riled up and told her we'd raised her to have faith, and if she couldn't trust God for the hard times, she didn't have no faith at all. Boy, did she get me riled up!"

"Yes, sir, I understand. Meg can raise a guy's temperature when that stubborn streak of hers shows itself. Then what happened?"

"I told her she had some business to do with God, and she'd better go to her room and talk to her heavenly Father, because her earthly father couldn't help her with this one."

"You didn't show her any mercy, did you?"

"No, I didn't. After that, we didn't talk about it anymore. The next morning her eyes were swollen, and she looked like she was half sick, but I saw peace in those eyes. I'm sure hoping God got through to her. Imagine her thinking the woman we both adore is a burden to me. It's unthinkable!"

"Do you think she'd agree to marry me if I went to see her?" James asked.

"I don't know, but when she left, she hugged me and told me thank you for everything. I hope she got it worked out with God. It's out of my hands now and between you two and God. I'll tell you this, though. There's no one I'd rather give my Meg to than someone who loves her and the Lord as much as you do."

"I wish I knew what to do," James confessed.

"I think you better ask the Lord about that. He's got the answers, not me. If God wants you two together, He'll give you wisdom and let you work things out."

Meg heard the phone ringing but tried to ignore it by turning over and hugging the pillow to her ears. "Why won't they give up?" she groaned out loud. "I don't want to talk to any of my students in the middle of the night." Slowly, she pulled herself out of bed and grabbed her phone.

"Good morning, Aunt Meg," a cheery voice said.

"Bill, it's three in the morning. Oh! Bill! Do we have a baby? You called me Aunt Meg."

"Now that you're finally awake, I'll tell you we have a fine boy—Caleb Andrew." He gave Meg the infant's statistics and told her proudly that he and his son shared the same hair color. Caleb had arrived just an hour earlier. "Am I forgiven for waking you up?"

"You bet you are! I won't be able to go back to sleep, though, because I'm too excited. I'm glad you kept his gender a secret, but now I know what to buy for him. How's Sherry?"

"She did well, but I could hardly stand her pain. It nearly killed me to see her hurting so much, but she insisted she wanted to experience a natural birth."

"If you thought it was hurting you, what do you think it was doing to her?"

"I got to be with her the whole time. The miracle of birth was the most amazing thing I've ever seen in my life. Just wait till you see Caleb 'cause I know you'll agree he's something special."

"Bill, is he really okay? You know … ah … does he have what Mama has?"

"It's too early to tell. We'll love him either way it goes."

Meg, true to her prediction, did not go back to sleep. She planned a shopping trip to get her nephew a few things and then got dressed for school. She continued to thank God for Caleb's safe arrival and prayed he would stay disease free.

After school, she hurried to the mall to shop for baby things. There were so many things she wanted to get, but she didn't know what Caleb had already. She found a shirt that read "I love my aunt," so she had to purchase it and little pants to match. It made no difference that the outfit was a size 2. He would wear it someday.

Three weeks later Bill called again. "Say, big sister. Do you want to meet your nephew?"

"I can hardly wait to see him. Are you coming to see me?"

"We're going to take him to Mom and Dad's. They're most eager to meet their first grandson, and we're just as eager to show him to them. Could you go visit them the same weekend we go? I know you usually don't go until Easter."

"In order to get to meet my nephew, I will be there."

"How about this weekend?" Bill asked.

"I've got to take a group of students to a contest. Could you wait until the next weekend?" Meg asked.

"Sure, we can do that. That will give Sherry and Caleb another week to get into the swing of things. Maybe by then he'll decide he should sleep all night instead of wanting to be fed twice every night. Let me tell you something; being a parent is not for wimps. Sherry and I are exhausted."

When word reached Mitchell Green that his children were coming for a visit, he decided it was time to drop by to see his pastor. He walked into the church and saw the pastor's office door was standing open, so he walked right in to speak to James. "Do you want to go to lunch with me? I'll buy," he said to James.

"I can't refuse an offer like that. Give me about twenty minutes to finish what I'm working on, and I'll meet you at the café."

Once the order had been placed, James asked the question he knew would keep Mitchell talking for a while. "How's that new grandson?"

"That's why I asked you to lunch. They're coming to see us next weekend. I knew you and Bill went to seminary together, so thought you'd like to know."

"Do you suppose Bill would say a few words for us? I'm sure our folks would love to hear from the hometown boy."

"Call and ask him. He'll tell you if he doesn't want to. He might still be on such a cloud from having the baby that he can't get two words to come together," the older man laughed.

"I'll do just that. Have you got his phone number on you?" James asked.

"One more thing you might want to know. Meg's coming too."

"Praise God! I won't have to wait until Easter to see her. Have you told her I'm your new pastor?"

"Nope. Figured if you wanted her to know you were here, you'd tell her yourself."

"I haven't contacted her. I've prayed about it and just can't get the peace I need to make that phone call."

"Like I said, we haven't told her you are the pastor. We promised you we wouldn't. But we did tell her we thought our new pastor was pretty special and was sure she'd like him." Mitchell laughed as he relayed the information. "I can't wait to see her face when she sees you come to the podium." Mitchell said he would call her that night. "I'm going to tell her we've invited the new pastor for Sunday dinner too. It will be really funny. I can see her bristling because we're inviting a stranger to our family gathering." Mr. Green was obviously in a very good mood.

"Mitchell, will you pray I'll do and say just the right things to Meg? I love her, but we both have to know that being together is God's perfect plan for us."

He nodded at his pastor. "Son, I've been praying since we

talked. After I shared with Mama, she's been praying too. Let me tell you when that wife of mine prays, things happen. Anyway, we've grown mighty fond of you. We want God's best for you and Meg."

James found himself praying often in the days to come. He knew Meg was going to be shocked when she saw him at church. He didn't know how far she had come in her relationship with the Lord, but he prayed God had loosened the cloak of fear that wrapped itself around her. If only he could convince her how much he loved her, she'd know she would not need to worry about being handicapped—if she ever was.

"He's beautiful, absolutely beautiful," Meg declared with the pride of a close relative. "It was worth the drive to meet you, Caleb," Meg crooned as her nephew slept through her proclamations. Bill and Sherry beamed beside her as they shared the joy of introducing their son to his aunt and grandparents.

"It's my turn," Mitchell chimed in. "You and Mama have held him so much I haven't even had a chance to spoil him."

"Your chance will come when he's old enough to go fishing at the pond with you. Besides, you don't want to disturb his sleep. He's so comfortable now," Meg reasoned. Meg knew she had won and sat down in the rocker to enjoy her nephew.

"You cheat, young lady. When he wakes up, I get a turn."

Sherry decided she'd better settle the disagreement. "Grandpa, he'll be all yours, including his diaper change."

"Guess I'll show you folks a thing or two. I haven't forgotten how to change a diaper—at least I hope I haven't."

The Green household was in a tizzy to get to Sunday School on time. Three extra adults and a fussing baby made the morning a bit stressful, but all finally were ready to go.

"We can all ride in the van," Mitchell volunteered.

"I'm going to drive Sherry and me, so we can put Caleb in his car seat. He's so fussy this morning, the nursery workers probably won't want to keep him."

When Mitchell called to Meg that they were ready to go, she hurriedly finished the last touches to her hair.

"You're going to turn heads today," Bill assured her.

Sarah looked at her only daughter. The blue cotton dress was casual but dressy and made her eyes sparkle. Her hair shone as it hung loosely around her shoulders. With her three-inch heels adding to the femininity, Sarah thought James would find her daughter totally irresistible. However, she wasn't going to give Meg a hint who their new pastor was. Meg would find out soon enough. Mitchell and Sarah had prayed often about their daughter's fear of the disease her mother had. They, too, had reached the point where they could turn their daughter over to the Lord on this issue. If God wanted Meg and James to be together, He would work things out between them. The issue was beyond the reach of her loving parents.

Mitchell chuckled when he saw Meg leave the house and come to the van.

"What's so funny, Dad? Do I have something out of place?" She glanced at her dress and shoes, and everything seemed to be in order.

"I was just thinking, you're going to be a sight to behold for long-empty eyes."

"Those who haven't seen me for a while might be surprised that your little Meg has grown into a woman," she replied not knowing her dad was talking about James.

Mitchell was lowering the loading ramp of the van for Sarah's wheelchair and whispered to her, "I hope I get to see her face when she spots James. Let's try to keep her away from our new preacher until worship time, shall we?"

Sarah agreed, and they shared a look only those deeply in love would recognize as a hidden message.

Since the Green family was barely on time, Meg hurried to a young adult Sunday School class. Sarah wheeled toward her room, greeting those who also were running a little late.

James saw Mitchell and motioned for him to come speak with him.

"How's it going, son?" Mitchell greeted his pastor.

"Come into my office." When Mitchell seated himself, James confessed, "It's been hard to stay home, knowing Meg was at your house, but I just didn't feel I should come over to see her. I've been working on my sermon and praying for wisdom."

"Meg asked me why we had to have the preacher for dinner this weekend when we had so little time together as a family. I assured her you would fit in fine and changed the subject. She was slightly perturbed, I think, but tried not to let it show much. Usually Meg is so generous to others, but I guess she wants to keep Caleb just to the family on his first visit."

"Let's pray I fit in fine."

Although Mitchell felt James was a bit anxious about the visit, he took his statement seriously and prayed earnestly for the relationship between his daughter and his pastor.

<hr />

As the service began, Meg was turned in her pew, visiting with a friend from high school. As the first hymn was announced, she faced the front of the sanctuary and was visibly shaken when she saw that James was her parents' new pastor! She looked directly at him. He smiled, nodded his head in recognition, and picked up a hymnal.

Mitchell, sitting next to his daughter, whispered, "Is it okay that the preacher is coming home with us for dinner today?"

She nodded her head and her eyes misted.

James couldn't stare at her, since he had to perform his duties as pastor, but the next time he glanced at her, he saw that her face was glowing. *Lord, help me*, he prayed from his chair. *I will never make it through this sermon if you don't help me.*

Meg bowed her head, also obviously in prayer. Her prayer was different from the one James had prayed. She was thanking God that at last she was allowed to see James again. She asked for an opportunity to tell him how much she loved him and prayed that he still loved her. When she raised her head, she looked at James and smiled.

James had been preaching a series of sermons from Ephesians and was amazed to realize this week's message was on husbands and wives. How like the Lord to put the perfect topic before him for the sermon on this day. "Husbands are to love their wives," he began. He looked directly at Meg. "Today some people take lightly their wedding vows when they promise to love in sickness and in health. Scripture states a husband is to love his wife so much that he would give his own life for her. That does not mean deserting her if there's a crisis or an illness." As he spoke, his eyes stayed locked with Meg's. She now realized James and her dad had talked about her, and she wanted to know more of his thoughts. "When I marry, I want my wife to know she will have committed love from me. I will love and cherish her in sickness and in health, in wealth or in poverty. She will be my soul mate and the love of my life. With the sincerity of my vows, will she marry me?"

His question was asked of the congregation and no one thought his words were out of the ordinary in the context of the sermon. Meg, however, knew they were meant directly for her. When James again looked toward her, she was nodding her head and smiling.

James didn't know how he got through the rest of that sermon, but somehow he did. If anyone would have asked him later what he said, he would not have been able to tell them.

After the benediction, the congregation began to exit, but they were not met by their pastor as usual. He had rushed to Meg. "Did you nod your head to mean you will marry me?" he asked excitedly.

"You'd better believe it! I've been praying for weeks that God would allow us to be together again. I was so wrong to send you away. When I saw you on the podium, I was awed at God's goodness to me."

James did not kiss her, but he did shout, "Ladies and gentlemen, before you leave, may I have your attention?"

Silence enveloped the sanctuary as all eyes turned in anticipation of what their pastor was going to say.

"Meg Green has just agreed to be my wife!"

Clapping burst out as well-wishers came to congratulate the happy couple. The congregation might have been surprised and pleased by the announcement, but no one was as happy as the young couple themselves. Only Meg's parents stayed back from the excitement, smiling in thanksgiving that their prayers had been answered.

Dinner at the Green house was a happy affair. James and Meg joined in all the conversations and shared some of the events that had brought them together as they worked at the resort.

"It's about time you two decided to tie the knot," Sherry told them. "Bill and I want you to be as happy as we are. We knew last summer that you two were crazy about each other, so we've been praying you would get past whatever was keeping you apart."

"You should have seen James' reaction when he first visited us and saw Meg's picture," Mitchell shared with his children. Looking at Meg, he added, "He talked about you all the rest of the day."

"Was I obnoxious?" James asked as he rose from his chair. "Meg, let's go for a walk. Your folks are picking on their future son-in-law," he said with obvious affection for the older couple.

Walking hand-in-hand, James and Meg headed toward the pond. As soon as they could no longer see the house, he took Meg in his arms and shared a long-awaited kiss. It held the tenderness and passion of months of prayer and longing for each other.

"I had almost given up hope I'd ever see you again. Then your dad brought me here to the pond to talk to me. He had guessed my love for you and wanted me to understand what you feared."

"Daddy's the one who made me come to my senses. When I told him I wouldn't risk saddling you with a cripple, he lit into me like a bull protecting his herd of cows. He informed me that Mama was not a burden to him, and because he loved her, it was his privilege to care for her. When I questioned him, he said there were times he was inconvenienced, but compared to his love for her, it was nothing. He was so mad at me that he sent me to my room like I was a ten-year-old. He told me it was time I talked to the heavenly Father. I was upset that Daddy didn't understand my position, but I did as he said. It took me most of the night, but I was finally able to trust God with my future health and our relationship. God showed me that I was being selfish when I refused to marry you, because I was denying not only my own happiness, but yours. That was when I began to pray that God would bring us together and prepare me to be the best wife I could be for you. I didn't write because I felt God would bring us together when the time was right."

As they kissed again, Meg knew her discourse was behind them, but a bright future lay before them. Sadly, who had travelled with Meg for the weekend, wagged his tail. Meg rested her head on James' shoulder as they relished being in each other's company. Even the atmosphere seemed to be content as they sat beside one another.

"When can we get married?" James asked.

"I'm under contract until the end of the school year."

"That's what I feared," he groaned. "My car is going to get a lot of miles on it, because I'm not waiting months or weeks to see you again."

With tentative plans made for a June wedding and trips to see one another, the two of them walked hand-in-hand back to the house.

Mitchell greeted them from the porch swing. "You two look like you've got things worked out between you."

"Daddy, would you walk me down the aisle in June?"

———

Bill Green stood solemnly at the front of the sanctuary as the wedding march began. Glancing at the face of his almost brother-in-law, he could see James was nervous and excited. As Meg began the walk down the aisle on her father's arm, James took one step forward to meet his bride.

Meg, radiant in a flowing gown of white satin and organza, was the symbol of virtue. Her beauty and serenity showed through her fingertip veil, as she had eyes only for her waiting groom. Mitchell lifted the veil and kissed his daughter good-bye. She would soon belong to another man.

The congregation had filled the church to overflowing. The community wanted to see their pastor wed a favorite girl of the area. No one was disappointed at the joy on their young pastor's face as his love radiated to his bride.

As they exited the church, Bert yelled, "Ya-hoo!"

Epilogue

STREETS GLISTENED WITH ice as the few cars foolish enough to be on them, slid their way to the inner-city mission. Controlling the vehicle was almost impossible, as James was learning.

Meg sat beside him in the passenger seat but was ready to brace herself in case they slid off the road. "I still think you should have canceled the service," she said.

They made it to church with only a few skids. Cassie, a dark-skinned beauty at five years old, fell as they walked the ice-covered sidewalk, but otherwise there were no accidents. James helped her regain her footing while Meg dusted the snow off their young daughter's coat.

Since the teens coming to the special service were able to walk the short distance to the mission, James was not concerned with the challenge it presented the kids who seemed to love anything adventurous. Snow wouldn't stop these kids.

Their own sons, Antonio and Juan, were among the teens anxious to join their friends and listen when their Uncle Bill spoke to the kids.

When the Puerto Rican brothers were adopted by the Greens five years earlier, the boys had not looked back at their years of struggle; their father had been killed in a drug war, and their mother died in a tragic car accident. James and Meg had adopted the boys and loved them as though they had been born to them. Cassie had been given to them by a thirteen-year-old unwed mother who wanted a better life for her child than she could give her.

Meg greeted Bill with the usual round of good-natured teasing between siblings. An inspiring speaker, he came to challenge the teens to dare to be different from their peers.

Sixty-two teens came into the building, complaining of the cold but laughing at the fun they'd had getting to the service. Evidence of a few snowballs still showed on the backs of some of them. They pushed at one another playfully as they took their seats. Faces filled with anticipation concentrated as Bill spoke.

"Who are you?" Bill began. "Are you going to be like your neighborhood, or is your neighborhood going to become like you? You can be a leader or a follower. You can stand for Jesus, or you can fall for anything. God don't make no junk. Be who God made you—something special. Give your life to Jesus and then get out there and conquer your neighborhood for Him!"

The teens cheered their speaker. "Yes, we can! Yes, we can!" they shouted.

James and Meg sat on the back row as the teens responded to the challenge. The couple saw former drug addicts, young prostitutes, and gang members getting excited about Jesus. They prayed many of their lives would change this night. They saw their own sons as inspired as the other kids. Cassie sat beside them, calmly coloring a picture.

Their dreams of an inner-city ministry sat before them.

Only God knew what the future held—maybe a larger family, perhaps a rescue mission and homeless shelter. They could trust God with their future regardless of what came.

To learn more about the life and works of
Velma Merritt, visit these sites:

www.velmamerritt.com
www.facebook/velmamerrittpublications

Lightning Source UK Ltd.
Milton Keynes UK
UKOW05f1530270614

234179UK00001B/27/P